**BBC**

# DOCTOR WHO

BBC CHILDREN'S BOOKS

UK | USA | Canada | Ireland | Australia
India | New Zealand | South Africa

BBC Children's Books are published by Puffin Books,
part of the Penguin Random House group of companies
whose addresses can be found at global.penguinrandomhouse.com

www.penguin.co.uk    www.puffin.co.uk    www.ladybird.co.uk

Penguin
Random House
UK

First published by Puffin Books 2012
This edition first published by Puffin Books 2016

001

Written by Gary Russell
Copyright © BBC Worldwide Limited, 2016

Printed in Great Britain by Clays Ltd, St Ives plc

A CIP catalogue record for this book is available from the British Library

ISBN: 978–1–405–92253–1

33614057703430

MIX
Paper from
responsible sources
FSC® C018179

BBC

# DOCTOR WHO

# HORROR OF THE

# SPACE

# SNAKES

## Gary Russell

PUFFIN

# Contents

# Chapter 1
# Travelling Man

The Doctor was in the TARDIS, standing in front of a tall mirror. He was gently swaying from side to side, swishing his new long green overcoat around.

'Good fit, yes?'

No response.

Of course not – the TARDIS was empty.

Amy and Rory were safely tucked up in their new home in twenty-first century Leadworth. He tried to picture Amy, out in the back garden, probably battling with a barbecue while Rory was off somewhere, perhaps whizzing around the Forest of Dean in that new sports car the Doctor had got him.

And River Song? Back in her cell at the Stormcage Containment Facility in the fifty-second century, most likely. Unless it was night-time, in which case she and a

1

younger version of the Doctor (or maybe a slightly older one, who knows) were probably out somewhere, dining in Paris, examining modern art in New York or painting the town a variety of shades of *rood* in Amsterdam.

Or perhaps they were in Cersis Major, climbing the golden rock faces. Or in Talusia, helping the Weavers and their web-sky-cities stay aloft. Or maybe even having a swift bottle of pop with Jim the Fish and his extraordinary family under the starlight on his waterworld.

The Doctor didn't want to think about what the dozens of other travellers he'd known and befriended over the years might be up to since leaving his TARDIS. That way madness lay.

No matter what face he wore, the Doctor never liked being alone in the TARDIS. And the TARDIS, he was convinced, disliked it equally. Somehow everything seemed a bit more sluggish, a bit slower to respond. The lights seemed a bit dimmer, the ambient temperature a few degrees cooler.

'I know,' he said to the time rotor as it rose and fell within its glass tubing. He stroked a few of the controls on the console, and blew some dust off the old record player he'd once restored after someone had chucked a spear into it.

He couldn't remember how or why or when that happened. Things like that tended to blur in his memory. Having companions aboard the TARDIS always kept things in focus; if someone had been there, he'd have been able to say the exact date and time it had happened, he'd have a point of reference, something to trigger the memory.

'Doctor,' he declared aloud to himself. 'Doctor, Doctor, Doctor, someone is getting a bit maudlin, and a teensy-weensy bit stir-crazy. Loneliness is all in the mind – there's a universe or ten out there to explore. Tell you what, Doctor, let's play Reckless Randomiser. That's always fun.'

He threw himself at the coordinate control panel and shut his eyes, simultaneously running the palms of his hands over all the switches, dials, touch-sensitive rollers and archaic levers and pulleys at once. Then he counted to ten, turned round four times and checked to see where he was heading next. Reckless Randomiser could be such fun.

He looked at the result.

'Typical.'

He pulled a switch and a planet appeared on the huge TARDIS scanner and on all the smaller screens dotted around the control room.

'Earth. What's random about that? Or reckless, to be honest.'

The Doctor felt a twinge in his head. 'Oww. Ow, ow and oww again,' he said, diving his hand into an inside pocket of his overcoat and pulling out the little wallet that contained his psychic paper.

He stared at it.

HELLO THERE. NEED HELP PLEASE. UNIT MOONBASE ONE. ARCHITECTS (AND BUDGET) GETTING OUT OF HAND. NEED SORTING BY THE MINISTRY. THANX. THE KOMMANDANT.

He thought about it.

UNIT – yup, knew them. Not always fond of them, but there had been a few golden moments.

The Moon – yup, that he knew too. Been there more than once – indeed, he'd been to Moonbase One itself a few times over the centuries. It had been used variously as everything from a weather-control system to a prison to a huge children's amusement park. Oh, that roller-coaster . . .

The kommandant, though? That meant nothing. No one he knew.

Occasionally, the psychic paper picked up messages not actually meant for him, sort of like picking up a foreign TV station when retuning the Digibox – or at

least that was how Rory had described it once. The
Doctor had agreed in principle even if he didn't quite
get the analogy.

This looked like one of those times. After all, what
did the Doctor know about architects? There was
something about Shadow Architects in his memory,
but he was pretty sure that wasn't the same thing
at all . . .

The TARDIS landed.

The Doctor threw a look up into the ether. 'Thank
you. Are you trying to tell me I need something to
occupy myself with? Well, all right. We'll nose
around for half an hour – just thirty minutes. Then
I'm coming back and we'll find somewhere really
random to go that you can't influence.'

As if in answer, the TARDIS lights glowed a bit
brighter.

With a sigh, the Doctor checked that the psychic
paper was safe in his trouser pocket, patted his top
pocket to make sure there was a Jammie Dodger
in it and, with a smile on his face, he exited the
TARDIS . . . and walked straight into a door. The
TARDIS had deposited him inside a *very* small
storeroom.

The Doctor reached out and found a wheel on
the door, which he turned with one hand. It was

rather difficult; the wheel was designed for two-handed turning, but since his right hand and arm were squashed between the TARDIS and the wall, that was not going to happen.

The door swung open – outwards into a corridor, luckily – and the Doctor heaved himself into the brightly lit space. Everything was varying shades of dull grey. Bland walls, bland floors and bland ceilings.

'Imagine if this place had some colour,' the Doctor muttered to himself. 'Some pictures pinned up, or some murals painted on the walls. Now that would be nice.'

The corridor followed a continuous curve, so the Doctor was unable to see any further than where the corridor turned just ahead of him.

Popping the Jammie Dodger in his mouth, he walked forward, keeping one hand close to his psychic paper, in case it was needed. Every so often he passed a UNIT insignia stencilled on a door; these military bods could often be 'shoot first, ask questions later' types, so he proceeded with caution.

As he followed the corridor round, munching on his biscuit, two men in black UNIT coveralls and red berets appeared and marched towards him.

'Here we go . . .' he said under his breath.

'Oh, there you are.' One of the soldiers smiled. 'We thought you'd got lost.'

The other soldier tapped his ear, activating some kind of bluetooth device. 'Greyhound Eighteen to Trap Six. We found him, kommandant.'

'Wasn't aware I was lost.' The Doctor smiled. 'My name is –'

'It's all right, Mr Moss,' the first soldier said. 'People often make a wrong turn up here and it can take an hour just to walk the circumference of the base. Not a problem. The others are waiting for you. This way.'

With a shrug, the Doctor let himself be marched along the curved Moonbase corridor, noting the various rooms and signs that he passed. One in particular intrigued him.

'What's HEART?' he asked.

'All will be explained by the American,' a soldier said.

'Ah, Americans, they know everything,' the Doctor joked. 'Or think they do.'

'That's right, sir,' replied the soldier in a neutral tone of voice that implied neither agreement nor disagreement.

A door opened behind them.

'Sergeant?'

The two soldiers and the Doctor stopped and turned. Both UNIT men saluted.

'Mr Moss, yes?' said the man in a German accent. He was looking at the Doctor, clearly believing he was this Mr Moss person. 'I am the kommandant. May I say I am very glad to have you up here.'

'My pleasure, kommandant,' the Doctor said. 'Your message sounded . . . urgent. I got here as fast as possible. Your lads here were marvellous at finding me, too. I got lost, I'm afraid.'

The kommandant looked the Doctor up and down.

Sensing a challenge to his sartorial elegance, the Doctor flicked his hair back a bit and tweaked his bow tie.

But the kommandant just smiled. Perhaps he was used to such . . . eccentricity in the civilians who visited the Moon every so often.

'Listen,' he said, 'if you can sort out Mr Galan, I'll be incredibly grateful. See what you think and, after your meeting, let's talk again. Sergeant Tanner?'

'Yes, sir?'

'Stay with the architects please and bring Mr Moss back to my office afterwards, would you?'

'Sir.'

The kommandant turned and disappeared back through the door from which he'd come.

Sergeant Tanner and the other soldier escorted the Doctor onward.

It occurred to the Doctor to wonder what he would do when the real Mr Moss turned up. Well, he'd cross that bridge when he came to it.

A few minutes later, the soldiers ushered him into a huge room with a high, domed ceiling, kitted out with foldaway chairs arranged in a circle round the walls. Many of the chairs were occupied by a mixture of civilians and UNIT personnel of differing ranks. In the centre of the room was a relief map of the Moon's surface, with the Moonbase at one side, and, standing beside this map, addressing his seated audience, was a tall man in glasses.

Next to him, a shorter man relentlessly tapped on a tablet, swiping away pages and doing that strange opening-and-closing finger movement that enlarged or decreased the size of images. They hadn't yet invented a proper word for that movement – though they would. The Doctor thought 'zooping' was a good option, mainly because three hundred years later he'd accidentally added it to the Galactic Humanish Dictionary without giving it a definition and this seemed as good an application as any.

So the short man continued zooping and the taller one continued talking.

Both were American, both had dull voices that made the Doctor sleepy, and both were talking a load of nonsense about the surface of the Moon, mapping its peaks and troughs and something about buying the dark side back from the Korean Unity, although no one knew how they owned it in the first place.

The Doctor just about said, 'Oh, that was me,' but stopped himself before he did so. He was remembering a game of draughts he'd won against Kim Someone-or-other back in the 1950s, which had meant that in ninety years' time the two Koreas would amicably become one and, in exchange, get real estate on the Moon. Or something. The Doctor had never been too sure of the details, as River Song had been there, causing trouble with one of the more pompous families, and they'd had to make a quick getaway.

Right now though, in the assembly area of Moonbase One, the Doctor thought it best to keep that one to himself.

He became aware of another person standing by the door, getting slightly in the way of Sergeant Tanner and the other guards: a small man in white coveralls, carrying a red toolbox. He looked like a maintenance worker, and appeared to be trying to fix a problem with one of the air vents at the point where the wall met the floor.

The Doctor watched the man unscrew the small vent, but couldn't quite see what he was doing. In fact, it seemed as though all he was doing was staring into the vent. He then replaced the grill, nodded to the soldiers and left. The whole exercise appeared to the Doctor to have been a waste of time.

'Bob?' called out one of the American voices. 'Bob?'

The Doctor realised that the two Americans were looking at him.

'You're Bob Moss, yeah?' the taller one asked loudly.

'Yes. Yes, absolutely. Bob Moss. Ministry of . . . Architects and Cartographers,' he said with a smile. 'Sorry I'm late.'

The Americans looked confused.

'Zeppatelli,' the tall one said, 'take Bob outside, and show him the lay of the land.'

The shorter man nodded and made his way over to the Doctor, holding out a hand to shake, which the Doctor did.

'C'mon, Bob,' Zeppatelli said. 'Galan can talk for hours, and we don't need to listen to his plans for the other Moonbases. I guess you've read the specs and schedules by now?'

'Oh, yes. Absolutely,' lied the Doctor. 'Nice to meet you after . . . so long.'

Zeppatelli frowned. 'Heck, it's only been three weeks since you emailed us.'

'Feels like forever,' the Doctor added quickly.

As they headed out of the big room, the Doctor stopped and eased Sergeant Tanner to one side very slightly so as to peer down at where the maintenance man had unscrewed the vent cover, then put it back.

Nothing. Nothing weird, or strange, or unusual. Nothing whatsoever, besides the fact that he had done it at all. Perhaps, the Doctor decided, that was mysterious enough.

Sergeant Tanner told them he'd lead them to the Suit Room, where they would get kitted up for a moonwalk, and that he was coming with them.

A few minutes later, they were seated in a small buggy, and Zeppatelli was driving it out across the dusty surface – a bit too fast for the Doctor's liking.

# Chapter 2
# New Sunshine Morning

26 June 2017

Lukas Minski watched as the door swung outwards, slowly but steadily. His heart was going ten to the dozen as he stepped through the doorway. It was his first time, and he was determined to enjoy it, fear and everything.

What he was doing was dangerous – no two ways about it. Each step was potentially lethal: a misstep here, a trip there, anything could kill him. In every square metre, there were more things that could kill him than could save him – something drilled into him from his earliest days in training. Not a nice thought,

but one he'd never forgotten. After all, no one wanted
a repeat of what had happened to Carlos.

He took a few steps forward. Ahead, he could see
the buggy with a group of three guys standing around
it, waiting for him. In his hand, he carried his red
toolbox, all he needed to justify what he was doing
there.

He eventually made it to the buggy and could
see straight away what the problem was: one
of the wheels had hit a rock and twisted the rear
axle.

'That is a big job,' he explained.

'Really? I hadn't noticed,' said the American who
Lukas knew was the driver. Arrogant man, but good
at his job. He was an architect and responsible for
what were currently referred to as 'the lower levels',
usually in a tone of voice that suggested they were
somehow scary and threatening. They weren't. They
were exactly what their name said: lower levels.
Architects always liked to exaggerate their own
importance.

'What speed you were going?'

'Who cares,' said one of the others. That was the
UNIT man – he wore sergeant stripes on the arm of
his spacesuit. Lukas tried to remember his name, but
without success. 'Can you fix it?'

'Yes, sir, but it is taking me maybe a couple of hours. I am new to this. You are better to go in and wait, yes?'

The three men looked at Lukas. He could tell from their limited body language that they weren't happy, but there was nothing to be done. If they'd driven the buggy less recklessly, they wouldn't have this problem, would they?

Two of them walked off immediately, but one hung back.

'You going to be all right out here alone?' he asked Lukas in an English accent. 'Your first week, yeah?'

Lukas assured him that he'd be fine. 'My first job actually out here,' he said proudly, holding up his toolbox. 'This was gift from Darya, my wife. New tools for new career.'

'A new career, Mr . . . ?'

'Minski. Lukas Minski,' Lukas said. 'I worked in UNIT museum in Georgia – lots of treasures and pictures. Very pretty, but often sad stories. The museum, it was full of things it should not have, things not belonging to it,' he said. Then he coughed, as if realising he was rambling. 'But I grow bored, all day watching fat, rich people stare at things they do not understand. I like to use my hands, so Darya say it was time to do something new.' He laughed. 'Never argue with the wife, yes?'

The Englishman nodded. 'Absolutely. I've tried arguing with mine, and all that ended up doing was changing the entire history of the universe. More than once, I imagine.'

Lukas stared at the man, but couldn't see his face through the visor. 'Okay . . .' he said carefully. 'So now I am working with my hands, mending things, making everything work, from the lights to the cars. I believe you English say I "get to the heart of the matter", no?'

The Englishman laughed. 'I'm not really English, Lukas. I just do the accent.'

Again Lukas, unable to see the man's face, couldn't be sure how serious he was being. He bent down and tapped a six-digit code on the red toolbox's lock and it sprang open.

'Security,' he said. 'Have to keep my tools safe, yes?'

The Englishman was watching Lukas intently – he could feel his eyes on him even through the darkened visor.

'Absolutely,' the Englishman said. Then he pointed to a photo glued into the underside of the toolbox lid. It showed a blonde woman and a small blonde girl, very austere, dressed in black and standing in front of a church.

'Family?' he asked Lukas.

Lukas glanced down at the photo. 'Anni's birthday is next week. She is to be ten. She is wanting to have big party, but I do not think so now. This is making me sad. She is reason for everything I do.'

Lukas glanced up. The Englishman seemed to be staring across the path where the buggy had stopped, his hand raised to try to keep the sun off his polarised visor.

'What is problem?' Lukas asked.

'Dunno,' the Englishman said. 'Thought I saw movement.'

Lukas stood up. 'What kind of movement? No one else is scheduled to be here?'

'No, it wasn't people. It was like . . . oh, well, doesn't matter.'

Lukas frowned. 'Seriously, what is problem?'

The Englishman shrugged. 'You'll think I'm mad.'

'You work here,' Lukas laughed. 'Of course you are mad! We all are, to be up here.'

But the Englishman wasn't laughing. 'You know that movement you see in those nature documentaries – those snakes that move sideways in a sort of S shape?' He made the movement with his gloved hands.

Lukas laughed. 'You see snakes out here? Sidewinders? Here?'

The Englishman put his hands up in mock surrender. 'Yeah, okay. Must be the sunlight creating mirages or something. Anyway, I'll see you inside. I'll get Zeppatelli to buy you a drink to say thanks for fixing the buggy he's wrecked.'

Lukas smiled. 'Okay, yes, deal. I find you in the mess in ninety minutes or so.'

The Englishman tapped the side of his head with his finger in mock salute. 'Cheers, Lukas. See you later.'

Lukas watched him wander back to join his friends inside. As the door closed behind him, shutting him away from Lukas, the mechanic was pleased. He preferred working alone and in silence. He loved his machines, loved fixing them.

He had been building a small model of a moon buggy to celebrate his daughter's birthday. He knew it wasn't an ideal use of his free time, but shopping was . . . limited here, so home-made presents were the best you could get.

As he bent down to his toolbox, Lukas's eyes drifted towards where the Englishman had supposedly seen the strange movement and, for a second, Lukas saw something too. Perhaps it was a trick of the sunlight on the ground.

He turned his focus to repairing the ruined buggy axle.

Then he stopped again.

Something was there, he just knew it.

The trouble with spacesuits and their visored helmets was that they limited your vision. Lukas could look straight ahead and a bit to either side, but by the time he'd moved his entire body round in zero gravity whatever was behind him could have leapt up and grabbed him.

Nevertheless, he did turn round – and there they were.

Facing him. Thin, silvery creatures.

They were snakes much like the hooded cobras from Earth. Dark, sulphurous yellow eyes suggesting decay glinted and eyelids nictated back and forth, focusing in on him. The hooded heads rocked back, and one snake opened its mouth to reveal sharp fangs. But what was really freaky – other than the simple fact that there were snakes on the Moon – was that, unlike the multicoloured, scaled snakes back on Earth, these were metallic silver. Maybe it was the sunlight, maybe it was madness, but Lukas swore there was something about their skin that was, not robotic, but more like – no, that was impossible!

And the impossible was indeed facing Lukas Minski: space snakes.

Lukas wanted to laugh at the ludicrousness of it – but he didn't. Instead he reached towards his red toolbox. 'Not yet,' he said. 'Please, not yet . . .'

As one, the snakes lunged across the surface of the Moon towards him, so much faster than anything Lukas had ever seen before.

He threw up his hands to protect himself.

# Chapter 3

# Life in a Day

Three days later, the base kommandant was reading the report that Bob Moss had submitted before he had returned to Earth (it briefly registered in the kommandant's mind that no one had actually seen Moss go, but that didn't matter).

Moss had proven to be as good as the kommandant had hoped. He'd calmed the two Americans down, got them to stop trying to dominate meetings and also found ways to bring their plans in way under budget – so far under budget, in fact, that UNIT was considering a couple of other corporations that had submitted ideas which might be even more economically viable. Moss had been responsible for putting their tenders in front of the kommandant too. What a good man that Bob Moss was.

But for now he was more interested in this report, because it detailed the initial buggy accident and confirmed that Lukas Minski had reported at 14.25 CET to repair it.

The architect's team had returned to base but Moss had stayed outside with Minski a few more minutes. His report made mention of the strange phenomena he had seen on the ground, which he had referred to as 'snakes'.

The kommandant pressed the DELETE key, and all references to snakes were obliterated. It wouldn't be good to have that on anything official at this stage of development. And Moss had signed enough forms to ensure that he'd be locked up for years for breathing a word about this back home.

The kommandant saved the document and emailed it to HQ, naming it: FILE_LM/dec/Unexp.doc.

He attached the one photo showing the crashed buggy, with Lukas Minski's abandoned spanner sitting there beside it, next to a small, torn picture.

There was also another photo, which had been taken shortly afterwards and showed that the spanner was gone, but its shape was still indented into the dust – as it always would be. The spanner was now in lock-up, as evidence along with that photo.

The kommandant briefly glanced at the photo within the photo. It showed a woman and a young girl by a church. He checked his records – yes, Minski had a wife and daughter. With a heavy heart, the kommandant realised someone would have to tell them that their husband and father had vanished in an inexplicable manner and should be presumed dead.

They'd get his full benefits of course, but the kommandant knew that was really no consolation for Lukas's death.

Maybe he'd ask Bob Moss to go to their house and tell them. He was the last person to speak to Lukas. He could tell them his mood, tell them about the birthday and pass on the gift they'd found in Lukas's room.

Yes, Bob could do it – the English were good at things like that. The kommandant could always pull the old card: 'Oh you know us Europeans, we're never the best at breaking the sad news. People say we don't have the empathy.'

He noted that Minski's toolbox was missing from the evidence. It had been a red metal one, according to witnesses. The photo and spanner were left behind but Minski, or whoever was responsible for his disappearance, had taken the toolbox.

Why?

The kommandant shut down his computer and sighed.

Snakes indeed. *Space snakes*. On the surface of the Moon. How ridiculous was that?

He was interrupted by a knock on the door.

'Come.'

It opened and Sergeant Tanner saluted him.

'You look concerned, Tanner,' the kommandant said.

'We have an intruder, sir,' Tanner reported. 'At least, I think he is. He says he's here at your request.'

'Who is it?' The kommandant slid his computer into a drawer.

A small, balding man in a dark suit and carrying an attaché case pushed past Tanner and stood facing the kommandant.

'I must make a formal complaint, kommandant,' he said angrily. 'Since I got here, your troops have treated me like a criminal, accusing me of spying, of being an impostor and, most of all, refusing to believe my credentials. *You* asked me here, kommandant. *You* sort it out.'

The kommandant looked at Tanner with a shrug, then smiled at the angry newcomer. He was English – always so angry, the English.

'I'm very sorry, but I have no idea what you are talking about,' he said calmly. 'Who are you?'

The Englishman snatched a piece of paper that Tanner was carrying – presumably Tanner had taken it from him earlier.

'There,' he said. 'Look.'

It was an official UNIT docket, giving permission for him to come to the Moon and carry out tasks as required. It bore the kommandant's signature.

He glanced at the name at the top. 'Is this a joke, Tanner?'

Tanner shook his head. 'Sorry, sir, no idea.'

The kommandant looked at the angry man in front of him. 'And this is you, is it? You are Robert Moss, from the ministry?'

The man produced a photo ID.

'Yes, I'm Bob Moss,' he said. 'And you invited me here!'

The kommandant looked from Moss to Tanner. 'Then who the hell, Sergeant Tanner, was the Bob Moss who was in Moonbase One for the last few days?'

# Chapter 4

# **Great Leap Forward**

8 April 2025 (eight years later)

Sam took a deep breath and closed his eyes. Why was he first? That was weird. Surely one of the others, one of the grown-ups, should have pushed their way to the front, all cocky and confident. But they hadn't. They'd sort of let him take the lead this time. Great. Thanks, everyone.

And that voice he recognised came from the very back, but, because it was coming through a helmet speaker, it sounded like it was right next to him. Someone was telling him everything was fine and safe, provided he followed 'procedures'.

Sam found that really, really annoying. For a start, *which* procedures? As if anyone had actually been listening when the computer read them out.

Now the voice was suggesting oh-so-politely that he get a move on.

'Honestly, Sam, we really don't have all day. Literally. We have about six minutes,' said Joe Rivas.

The next voice Sam heard in his helmet was Caitlin's.

'You okay, Sam?'

Of course he wasn't okay. He was about to climb down from a space shuttle and stand on the Moon. *The Moon.* Big thing. In the sky. Up there! Well, not so 'up there' at the moment – more sort of 'three metres down below and looking very grey, dusty and a bit scary'.

'I'm fine,' Sam managed to reply. 'It's just a bit . . .'

'Yes, I perceive it is,' said another voice. That was Michael. Only he would say 'perceive' rather than 'know'. He was the brainy one, and he used long words whenever possible.

Sam tentatively put a foot on the ladder of the shuttle and felt it hard beneath him. With a deep breath he turned round so he was facing the others and began to lower himself away from the relative safety of the shuttle towards the surface of the Moon.

He felt rather than saw other feet on the ladder above him as he went down, their footsteps seeming heavier and more urgent than his. Obviously not as scared as him, then.

After what seemed like ages, but was probably fewer than thirty seconds, Sam reached the bottom of the ladder. He remembered what they'd said earlier: 'Just let go'. The gravity on the Moon meant it was possible to drop safely down to the ground, though that turned out to be easier said than done.

'Any chance you might let go?' said a voice in his helmet. That was Savannah. Sam always blushed when Savannah spoke directly to him. Thank goodness she couldn't see that while he wore the helmet. He obligingly let go and dropped a tiny distance on to the surface of the Moon.

*Wow.*

Savannah was suddenly standing beside him and then, one after another, Michael and Caitlin joined them. They stared at the ground, at the sky, at the shuttle and then across to Moonbase Laika.

'We're here,' Caitlin said in all their ears. 'We are actually here.'

Sam glanced back at the shuttle as the adults made their way down the ladder.

Hsui Lan was first, her national flag – the red square with five gold stars in the top left corner representing the People's Republic of China – emblazoned on her spacesuit along with the logo from *Catch A Star*, the international talent show she'd won last Easter. That logo was everywhere – on her t-shirts, her trainers, the shoulder bag in which she kept her tablet and, of course, her tablet's wallpaper.

Behind her was Aaron Relevy, the WebTube sensation who, at the age of ten, had so impressed multiplatform companies with his self-broadcast shows from his bedroom that one of them had hired him on the spot as a presenter and interviewer for youth programming. Now nineteen, he was already considered a veteran of broadcasting – and he was also the presenter of *Catch A Star*. His coming on the trip to the Moon was as exciting as it was obvious to Sam. It wasn't possible to imagine anything connected with *Catch A Star* not featuring Aaron.

Attached to the side of Aaron's head at all times was a home-made webcam, which broadcast everything he saw and heard back to the production base in London, where it would be cut into a series of reality shows for rapid transmission. Aaron had become famous the web over for the segment of his WebTube show in which he showed people how to build things out of discarded rubbish – he had built a mobile phone, a mini computer drive and a robot dog from bits he found in a rubbish skip at the back of an electronics shop. That one segment had brought him fame, fortune and the chance to host anything he wanted. *Catch A Star* had been his first choice, but it had actually been another one of Aaron Relevy's shows that had brought Sam and his other friends to the Moon.

Four months ago World State had announced that it was launching its first Lunar Transport Shuttle, affordable to all, for regular trips to the Moon. To mark this occasion, the webcast *BPXtra* had run a competition for kids to design a mural for the Chill-out Area (whatever that was) on Moonbase Laika. Split into two age categories, and with a prize for one boy and one girl in each age bracket, the winners would not only see their murals painted in the base but would also be the first people to make the public trip in the shuttle *Yerosha*.

Sam and Savannah were the winners in the thirteen- to sixteen-year-old group, and Caitlin and Michael were the winners of the nine- to twelve-year-old group.

Aaron Relevy had made the announcement on *BPXtra* one afternoon, and Sam had watched in shock with his mum and dad as the results were revealed.

'You're going to the Moon,' his dad had said quietly. His mum had just squealed in excitement.

His whole street had seemed to know within minutes and, before long, he was on the local news and the main page of the *Lichfield Times* website. The producers of *BPXtra* had arrived the next day, with forms for his parents to fill in, a list of dates when Sam would need to be at the old UNEXA training centre in Wolverton to get ready for the flight and a load of requests for appearances on *BPXtra* plus photo shoots with the other winners for various websites.

Now, as Sam stood on the surface of the Moon, staring across the vast distance to Moonbase Laika, he remembered one other thing that had happened, something he hadn't told anyone, including his parents, because at the time it had seemed so silly and, well, mad.

Sam had been in the *BPXtra* studio canteen with Caitlin and Savannah, getting to know each other and chatting about the training they were doing to get ready for the space flight. Sam had gone to a drinks machine, to get a can of cola, when an old man had walked over.

He looked harmless enough. At first Sam had thought he was a cleaner or something, and smiled at him. The man had stopped and leaned on the drinks machine, glancing around, like he was worried someone might see him. He stared at Savannah and Caitlin, who were chatting about some app on Savannah's smartphone, then brought his focus down to Sam's level, so they were eye to eye.

His face was lined, and his cheeks were red and blotchy. His scraggly hair was streaked grey and white, and looked like it hadn't been washed in weeks.

He took Sam by the shoulders. 'Listen to me. I do not have much time. They are watching and waiting. You be careful up there, young man,' he said, with a heavy European accent – Polish or Romanian maybe. His breath had been warm and stale, and Sam had flinched slightly. 'Look out for the red box. And the space snakes. They will be back for it.'

The man shook Sam's hand firmly and turned to walk away, but not before one last warning: 'Tell no one you saw me or they will be after you too. One day this will all be sorted and, finally, it will be time to go home.'

The man had then disappeared through a door, and a few seconds later Sam was being introduced to Aaron Relevy and Hsui Lan, who had been escorted into the room by some *BPXtra* staff. Sam had put it out of his mind.

Now, though, as he looked at the dusty surface of the Moon in front of him, he was sure that he had seen something move out of the corner of his eye. Maybe it was just the dust, stirred up by their arrival, but it had made Sam think of the bizarre sideways slithering of snakes moving quickly to avoid human contact.

Perhaps the old man had been right. Perhaps the space snakes were back. Whatever a space snake was.

# Chapter 5
# Cynical Heart

Sym Sergei was a bit of a technical genius. Back home in Ukraine, his grandmother had always said so. She loved her grandson and was not afraid of coming forward and telling everyone of his merits. People in the street, in the shops, local bloggers, anyone who would listen.

'Born on these streets,' she'd say. 'And now look at him. Trained in Moscow and America. By the Americans. He's been to MIT, even.'

Not that Sym was the first Ukrainian to have done so but, considering his grandmother had been brought up back in the late twentieth century, he had some sympathy with her excitement.

Sym was rather proud of himself, too, though he never liked to display it outwardly. He had been top of his class at MIT and had published enough papers to make him highly sought after. Going to the Moon had been a long-held ambition; he had grown up with his grandparents telling him about all those Russian cosmonauts who had been the first humans in space. When Moonbase Laika (named after a Russian dog sent into space almost seventy years ago) had been established by World State, it seemed that his destiny lay up here.

Within a week of receiving the news that World State had accepted him, Sym was settling into his small quarters on the base. He shared them with a Nigerian systems analyst called Hugo, and the two of them had hit it off straight away.

Sym was also an analyst but, while Hugo's speciality was spreadsheets and records, Sym's was artificial intelligences and programming. As a result he had been put on the Chief of Science's team, and was one of just three people on Moonbase Laika with 24/7 access to HEART – a huge responsibility, as the chief was forever reminding him.

HEART itself was a room at the centre of the base, connected to the outer ring by three long corridors. Between HEART, those corridors and the main base was just empty space.

He still remembered his first view of the base when his shuttle had landed on the Moon: a big dome with an outer ring at the bottom. But, once inside, he had learnt that under the dome everything wasn't quite so uniform. For a start there were three major areas: Command Area, the planetarium (with associated laboratories), and the mess. These three large rooms were equidistant from one another, with the ringed corridor entering each room on one side and exiting on the other. Along those corridors were storerooms, sleeping quarters, small hydroponic labs to create oxygen, and the filtration systems for food and water recycling.

At the centre of all this sat HEART, the place where Sym enjoyed spending as much time as possible.

HEART had three functions. Firstly, it was the literal nerve centre of Moonbase Laika. Life support, communications, all essential systems were adjusted and maintained by HEART. Secondly, it was a research device, constantly being updated with data that the labs sent it, formulating and distributing information and conclusions, satisfying World State's requirements that Moonbase Laika be a fully operational research station. And, thirdly, it was a records store – everything that had occurred at the base since it was first built right up to the present day was stored here, accessed via a series of encrypted codes that only the commander and immediate executive staff could access. Sym himself didn't have that clearance, but nevertheless was pleased to be one of HEART's operational team. It was a big responsibility but one he embraced.

HEART was a tall, cylindrical room, not especially wide but with walls that rose straight up, higher than anywhere else on the Moonbase. Small ladders placed at irregular intervals enabled an operator to reach a different level of controls. Right at the top, sixty metres up, was the small alcove which only the Chief of Science had clearance codes to go into – that was where the nuclear-power core was accessed.

Sym's job never required him to go much above thirty metres, but a few times he'd climbed all the way up just for the kick of looking back down. It was a long drop, illuminated by the ever-shifting pattern of glowing lights that HEART gave off. It was almost like the room was breathing, as the pulsating lights took on a rhythm if you stared at them long enough, and the best way to observe that was from above.

Right now, Sym was entering a new series of variables for HEART to consider. Recently a number of crewmen had suffered from amnesia. They'd either woken up in their beds unable to remember how they got there, or they would just wander into the mess or

Command Area, looking dazed after vanishing a few hours earlier.

No one had been able to explain how or why this was happening, but it was a matter of concern to Godfried, the Chief of Security.

Sym was seeing if HEART could detect a pattern to the disappearances or the people involved and uncover something that human eyes had missed.

He was just entering the exact times and dates of those occurrences when he heard the first sound: a sort of scratching that came from somewhere behind him.

He ignored it, assuming it was probably just some new noise made by HEART's programs as they chittered and buzzed away. Most people forgot it even made these noises after working there for a while; it all became white noise.

But there it was again.

Noticing it made him realise it couldn't be HEART, or his mind would have filtered it out.

There! Again!

The sound wasn't coming from inside HEART, but from Corridor Three, the one closest to the laboratory areas back in the ring.

Putting down his tablet, Sym stuck his head out of HEART and into the corridor. It took a few seconds for his eyes to adjust to the stark greyness of the corridor after the multicoloured haze of HEART.

He looked around.

Nothing.

No, wait. There it was again!

Sym was going to call out before reckoning that, even if anyone could hear him back in the ring, they'd probably think he was mad.

He looked around and heard the noise again. There. Down by the vent covering.

He dropped to the floor and put his face close to the vent, trying to peer into the darkness. He knew the vent system. It carried recycled air throughout the base in a series of small, thin tubes that laced under the surface of the base. The tech crews hated them; if anything went wrong, the vents were barely wide enough for a man to get his arm into, so all repairs and maintenance had to be done with remote-control devices small enough to travel through the networks.

The noise was definitely coming from the vents.

Was it a remote? One that had been left down there?

Unlikely – the tech guys were usually pretty good at tidying up after themselves.

*Hisssssss.*

What *was* that?

*Hisssss.*

Sym didn't like it at all.

Was air leaking? He put his hand on the vent grille but felt no pressure, so it wasn't a leak – thank God. If it had been and it wasn't dealt with within minutes, the whole Moonbase could be compromised. They might all die from asphyxiation as the air was sucked out of the base and into the vacuum of the surface.

But, if it wasn't a pressure leak, what could it be?

He reached into a pocket, took out a small screwdriver and released the grille.

A strange smell wafted into his nostrils and he coughed slightly.

That was weird.

With the grille gone, he could get fractionally closer and look downward slightly.

A flash of . . . silver? Something was moving down there!

But that really was mad.

Perhaps a remote-controlled device really had been left down there after all, picking up a stray signal and trying to move.

He reached into the tiny space with his hand, tapping into the darkness, trying to feel what the thing down there was.

He felt a stab of pain in his hand and whipped it back.

At first he assumed he'd caught the side of his hand on something jagged, but goodness knew what. As he looked at his hand, he saw there wasn't a scratch on it. Just two tiny marks, like pinpricks, about two centimetres apart. Slowly, blobs of blood oozed out of them.

He wiped the blood away and made to stand up and call a tech crew to deal with this. But he found he couldn't get up. His legs simply wouldn't push him upright and he realised he was lying on the floor, panicking.

Darkness rushed into his mind.

Sym's eyes closed and he blacked out.

# Chapter 6
# I Travel

Sam turned and watched the last people jump out of
the craft, an odd pair in their mid-twenties. They
worked for World State and, when not in spacesuits,
wore pristine pale blue suits, shirts and shoes. Like a
couple of cartoon characters, they had fixed smiles
that didn't reach their eyes. It was as if they had been
told to be as nice as pie to the kids but really would
rather have been doing anything else. Anywhere else.
With anyone else.

Sam could never shake the feeling that underneath
their chirpy smiles and 'hey, wow, kids, we're just as
excited as you are' attitudes, twins Joe and Jo Rivas
were hating every minute of this experience.

And that made Sam smile, because he didn't like
either of them. They were, they explained, there to
'protect the brand' which, after Caitlin asked for an

43

explanation, they learnt meant that World State considered the Lunar Transport Shuttle to be something big and important. 'It's like when you see a Batman movie or a James Bond film,' Jo had smiled insincerely. 'A big ongoing thing like that, with logos and names that people recognise the world over, that's a brand. And it's our job to make sure that everyone enjoys the brand and that what happens doesn't spoil it or disrespect it in any way.'

'That makes it crystal clear,' Savannah had sneered. 'Thanks for that.'

Michael had put his hand up and successfully caught Jo and Joe's attention. 'Yes?'

'Strictly speaking, Batman and James Bond aren't "brands". They are franchises,' Michael said. 'Ongoing movie series like that are –'

Joe had cut across him. 'Yes, well, it's all very complicated, I'm sure, but basically it means we have to make sure that nothing on this trip to the Moon reflects badly on either World State or, more importantly, our new, exciting and thrilling Lunar Transport Shuttle programme.'

Now, they all stood together at the airlock.

Sam recalled the schematics he'd seen on Moonbase Laika. It was basically like a huge bicycle wheel – the main area being the wheel, a long circular corridor. Along the way, the wheel had bumps – these were a series of important rooms, which he remembered included things like laboratories, canteens, and bigger places such as the Chill-out Area and the famous Command Area, which Michael had kept telling Sam he really wanted to see. Also on either side of the corridor were a series of cabins for the crew to sleep in. Then, leading from the wheel, were three long spokes, which led to a central hub that stretched upward. Sam didn't know what that central area was, though – it wasn't labelled on the schematics.

Excited by what was about to happen, what they were all about to see, Sam smiled as Joe reached forward and pressed a large green square on the wall.

*Perhaps it's the doorbell*, Sam thought.

Sure enough, a moment later, the outer door to the airlock opened with a big hiss, which they were able to hear through their suits, until the vacuum of space deadened the sound completely. They filed in and the door closed again.

'Four minutes,' Jo said inside their helmets. Sam knew that was how long it would take for the cubicle they were in to be filled with oxygen, after which time they would be able to take off their suits.

It was a very slow four minutes during which no one said very much. Aaron made a joke about the decor (it was grey, a lot of grey) and Caitlin asked if World State was planning trips to Mars, to which Jo laughed quickly and said Caitlin was a very clever little girl for asking such a very clever question. No actual answer though.

Sam focused on the hiss as the air seeped into the cubicle, knowing that once it stopped hissing it was just a further minute from being time to get out of their suits.

It was actually a minute and a half before Jo and Joe said they could remove their helmets and spacesuits, presumably just making sure. After all, Sam guessed, it wouldn't do their brand much good if they killed four kids and two web celebrities by suffocating them before they'd even got through the door of the Moonbase.

Joe Rivas turned a huge plastic wheel in the centre of the inner door to open it – the door reminded Sam of the ones he'd seen on submarines in movies.

Sam and the others got their first view of the interior of Moonbase Laika. It was exactly the opposite of what Sam had expected. He had imagined futuristic white corridors, carpets, hexagonal designs on the walls, maybe plants in red plastic vases.

But it looked nothing like the movies he'd watched in preparation. This was the long curved corridor – the 'wheel' he'd seen on the schematics – but it was so . . . sterile.

Basically Moonbase Laika was mostly bland steel and plastic girders holding pale blue squares in place that acted like big building blocks.

*A Lego Moonbase*, he thought, *where everything is curved so you can only see the next few metres ahead even if you keep moving.*

Jo and Joe Rivas almost seemed to melt into the walls, the blue of their suits and the walls being identical. Branding, he guessed.

They marched off down a corridor, in the same direction as a lit-up sign with a pointing red arrow and the word MESS.

Sam turned to Savannah. 'Exciting, yeah?'

She nodded, her eyes glittering as she took it all in.

Behind them, he could hear Aaron and Hsui passing comment about the place, while just ahead Michael was walking between Jo and Joe. He was pointing things out as they passed, displaying an amazing amount of knowledge about how this was constructed, or why that was shaped the way it was, or how the original plans for the base had changed because of this, that and the other. Sam liked Michael because, although he rarely shut up, he did know about stuff. Then there was the fact that it also probably annoyed the Rivas twins, as he clearly knew more than they did.

After a while they found themselves outside the mess, which Sam now realised meant 'canteen'.

'Okay, people,' Joe Rivas started, then stopped. 'Umm, where are Aaron and Hsui?'

Sam noticed that the web stars weren't with them. Joe threw his sister a look that might have been saying, 'Whose job was it to keep an eye on these people?'

She smiled at them. 'I expect they've seen something interesting that we missed. I'll go find them, while Joe takes you in for a . . . fizzy drink.'

'They probably won't have carbonated drinks on Moonbase Laika,' Michael explained to her. 'The atmospheric displacement means that –'

'Whatever.' Jo smiled slightly more tightly. 'You lot go in and settle down. I'll find the other two.'

Sam and Michael, however, chose to follow her – canteens were so boring, and Sam wasn't hungry. He wanted to see more of this place, and he knew Michael was thinking the same way. They followed Jo as she walked back down the corridor, but they didn't get very far before voices floated towards them.

'So, what – you just started strumming a guitar and making up songs about comic books?' said a man's voice Sam hadn't heard before.

'That's right.' That was Aaron. 'Put it up on the web and got four million hits in the first week.'

'Wow,' said the newcomer, as Aaron, Hsui and he came round the curved corridor. 'I'm impressed, and I'm not easily impressed. Unless you can do that magic trick where you put a phone inside a beer bottle. Now *that* is impressive – and I've never worked out how to do it.'

The newcomer was tall, dark-haired and quite young, although he wore an old-fashioned jacket and bow tie. He waved his arms around when he talked, wriggling his fingers all the time.

He glanced towards Sam, and it seemed that he was looking straight at him. He had the most amazing blue eyes, which glistened with something indefinable that made Sam grin.

'And you? Hsui, was it? Loved your album – the one with the picture of the swans on it.'

Hsui looked at him, confused. 'But it's not out yet. We haven't even revealed the cover to anyone.'

The newcomer made an exaggerated 'oh' look with his face. 'Sorry,' he said. 'My mistake.'

'The cover will have swans on it, though,' she said. 'How did you know?'

The newcomer shrugged. 'Oh, lucky guess, I expect. You look like a swans kind of girl, and people like swans . . . I think. Hope. Imagine. Probably.'

'Who are you?' Jo Rivas asked.

The newcomer produced a small wallet with some kind of ID in it. He was too far away for Sam to see what it said, but he heard the reply. 'Ministry of Moons and Moonbases. Very new. Very exclusive. Been sent here to check up on things, make sure everything is hunky-dory and that the, ummm, yes, the children here have a safe and educational tour.' He smiled at them all again, then leaned towards Jo. 'I assume education plays a part in all this? It's not all ice cream and fizzy pop?'

With an exaggerated sigh, Michael started again. 'They can't have carbonated drinks because –'

'Yes, yes,' said the strange man. 'Atmospherics and all that. Complete nonsense, of course. Provided the gravity is set correctly, nothing to stop you having lemonade, cola or ginger beer to your heart's content, actually.' He was close enough to nudge Michael's shoulder now, which he did playfully. 'But ten out of ten for knowing about such things. You are going to be very useful to me, I reckon.' He looked at the rest of them. 'You all are, I'm sure.' He then leaned forward and pointed back at the Rivas twins with his thumb. 'Except I'm not sure about the blue suits here. They look a bit grumpy to me.'

Joe Rivas stepped forward. 'Excuse me?'

'Doctor,' he said. 'I'm the Doctor. From the Ministry of –'

'I heard,' said Joe. 'Now, look, I – what are you doing?'

The Doctor had dropped to the floor and Sam was surprised to see him tapping at a small air vent between the wall and floor. He even seemed to sniff it. Then, as if he had suddenly remembered the others were there, he stopped sniffing, looked up at everyone and grinned rather sheepishly. 'What were you saying?'

'That I didn't know you were going to be here,' said Joe.

'Oh. Well, sorry. But that's not really my fault. Should have been on your itinerary.'

'What itinerary?' asked Jo.

'Well, there you are then,' smiled the Doctor, as if that solved everything. 'I was on the itinerary you don't have. See how easily things fall apart without itineraries and plans and stuff?'

Sam found himself grinning at the way this Doctor managed to poke fun at the Rivas twins without actually being rude to them.

'So, come on then, let's get this party started,' the Doctor said. 'Lead on.'

Jo Rivas raised her eyes to the ceiling, took a deep breath and then shrugged. 'This way,' she said.

As they re-entered the mess, Sam looked the Doctor up and down, and the Doctor in turn looked down at Sam, and winked. 'Hello. Excited to be in outer space?'

Sam nodded. 'It's brilliant,' he said.

The Doctor grinned. 'You know what, it is, isn't it? The most brilliant thing ever.'

'What were you doing, sniffing at that vent?'

'Oh,' said the Doctor. 'Oh, you noticed me doing that.'

Sam shrugged. 'Kind of think we all did.'

The Doctor pointed down at another vent. 'Air vents. For recycled air. Useful on a Moonbase.'

Sam agreed. 'But why the sniffing?'

The Doctor stared at Sam, as if making his mind up whether or not to tell him something – something

Sam had a feeling might be very important. 'I'm testing a theory that's been bugging me ever since I arrived here a couple of hours ago. Something on the tip of my –'

'Tongue?'

'No,' replied the Doctor. 'Tip of my mind. She can be so frustrating sometimes. Never tells me anything.'

'She?' asked Sam.

'The TARDIS. My ship. She gets a bit moody sometimes and presumably brought me back here for a reason. No real idea what, though. Have you?'

'Nope,' Sam said.

The Doctor wandered over to a porthole in the wall. Before following him, Sam dropped down to the vent and gave it a sniff. Nothing weird there, so perhaps – but, wait!

But that was impossible.

'Intriguing, isn't it?' asked the Doctor, without actually looking at Sam.

Sam immediately scurried over to join the Doctor, who was looking outside at the expanse of greyness that was the Moon's surface.

'What did the vent tell you?' he asked Sam, still not looking at him.

'I . . . but . . . nah, it's stupid.'

The Doctor looked at Sam with something like disappointment on his face. 'Oh,' he said. 'Oh, okay.'

Sam didn't want to disappoint this strange man. 'I heard . . . sounds.'

'What sort of sounds?' the Doctor asked, his face lighting up again in interest.

Sam shrugged. 'Just noises. Like something moving. Breathing, perhaps? But that's impossible. Nothing can be living in an air vent, can it?'

'On Moonbase Laika?' asked the Doctor. 'No, no, course not. Unless . . .'

'Unless what?'

'Unless it can.'

Sam glanced back at the vent, slightly alarmed by the Doctor's words.

Changing the subject, the Doctor drew Sam's attention back to the surface of the Moon. 'What do you see out there?' he asked.

Sam shrugged. 'Dust. The shuttle. Umm, more dust. And Earth floating in space.'

'Amazing,' the Doctor said. 'Look over there, that large crater, slightly deeper than the others. That's Armstrong, named after the first human to set foot here on this satellite.'

Sam smiled. 'I bet it's great to have craters named after you.'

The Doctor nodded. 'It's great the first few hundred times. And the second few hundred. And the . . . well, anyway, it never gets boring.'

'It must have been great to be Neil Armstrong. "One small step for man" and all that.' Sam recalled seeing the footage on the web, all grey and grainy but so awesome.

'Nice man, very smart and no ego,' the Doctor said. 'We had blueberry muffins once. He will always live on in history. So will Buzz Aldrin, immortalised in all those photos that Armstrong took. And Michael Collins, the first man to get furthest away from Earth, the first to see the dark side of the Moon. Fantastic achievements, all three. Not to mention all the others who followed. But those three were the lunar pioneers that made this place possible.' The Doctor sighed, then pointed once more out of the window. 'Now, shall I tell you what else I can see?'

Sam stared harder. There was nothing else to see.

'Each grain of dust just sits there,' the Doctor said. 'Unmoving, untouched even by solar winds. Just over there, protected by a small plastic dome, is Neil

Armstrong's footprint. And off to the left is a crater where the UNIT cosmonauts who built this base started measuring the Moon. The compass that one of them dropped is still there, on its end. And then, oh, just look at that dust. You see grey. I see colours, millions of different shades, each grain of dust telling a story about history, about the formation of the solar system, the whole universe. Some of them have been telling that story for millions of years, but no one ever listens.' He paused, then looked back at Sam. 'I'm just talking rubbish,' he said. 'Ignore me.'

But Sam was captivated. If he squinted, he was sure he could see silver and blue and green in the dust rather than just grey. And he was thinking about the footprint and the compass.

'It's beautiful,' he breathed. 'It's the Moon!'

The Doctor grinned broadly. 'Oh, I like you, whoever you are.'

'Sam. Sam Miller.'

The Doctor shook his hand. 'Good to meet you, Sam Miller. You and I are going to be good mates, I reckon.'

The Doctor wandered over to the others and Sam threw one last look outside on to the magical surface of the Moon.

And then, just for a brief second, he thought he saw something move. Just slightly, as if some of that space dust had shimmered and shifted.

*It was probably just light reflecting*, Sam told himself. After all, nothing was alive out there. Was it?

Once more, Sam found himself thinking of the old man's warning about space snakes. He thought about the vents, the noise, the breathing, the Doctor sniffing.

He looked outside again, but everything seemed still and untouched. Just as it had been forever.

Because nothing could live on the surface of the Moon. Especially not snakes.

# Chapter 7

# Let the Children Speak

Sam and the others were in the mess, drinking some strange fruit drink. It had little taste, despite the fruits painted on the label and the promises of nutrition, energy and vitamin C.

Sam chucked his into a box marked WASTE, and nearly jumped out of his skin when it was all but sucked out of his hand by a fierce gust of noisy wind.

'Ah,' said Michael. 'Vacuum disposal chutes. They take the waste and shred it into powder.' He smiled at Sam. 'Don't fall in after it.'

'I won't,' said Sam, gingerly moving away from the chute.

Jo and Joe were tapping on their smartphones; at first Sam had thought they were playing a game, but he soon realised they were messaging people – perhaps someone else on the base, or maybe World State HQ back on Earth. It occurred to Sam that they might also be checking up on the strange Doctor from the Ministry of Moons and Moonbases, when both the Doctor and Savannah walked into the café.

'Toilets are that way,' Savannah said, as if to explain their absence.

'Vacuum?' asked Michael.

Savannah nodded slowly in a way that suggested she hadn't been expecting toilets quite so ferocious.

Aaron and Caitlin were reading some notices on the wall – some were electronic, while others were written by hand and attached with some kind of sticky plastic material.

'Apparently some of our murals are going in here,' Caitlin said, frowning.

'Well, that's nice,' said Hsui. 'Brighten this place up no end.'

'I wanted them to go in the Chill-out Area,' said Caitlin. 'That's what *BPXtra* promised.'

'No they didn't,' responded Jo Rivas, putting her own drink carton in the waste carefully, having seen Sam's surprise earlier. 'They just *hoped* they might be.'

'Still,' said the Doctor cheerily, looking at each child in turn. 'Could be worse. Could be the toilets they put them in.'

Jo and Joe Rivas threw him a look as if to say, 'Great, that helps,' then went back to their phones.

'Well,' the Doctor continued, 'shouldn't someone from the base have met us by now?'

'Just what we're checking on,' muttered Joe.

Aaron sidled over to Hsui.

'You okay?' he asked.

Hsui nodded and Sam noticed she seemed to turn away slightly, staring briefly at the tabletop, the ground and then finding a salt-shaker quite interesting – anything to avoid catching Aaron's eye. It had become obvious to everyone that Aaron fancied Hsui, and that Hsui fancied him – but they were both too shy to actually say anything to each other.

The presenter seemed to be getting braver though. 'Fancy a quick wander?'

'Sounds like fun. I'll come with you,' said Sam.

'No,' said Aaron.

'Yes,' said Hsui at the same time.

'Okay,' said Aaron, shooting Sam a look that immediately made Sam wish he'd not said a word – and Sam realised that they probably wanted to be alone. But it was too late to take it back now.

'Actually, no, you can't,' said Joe. 'Everyone, stay here. We can't go wandering around Moonbase Laika like we own the place.'

'I thought you did,' said Caitlin. 'World State, anyway. And you are from World State.'

'We work for World State,' Jo said. 'Not the same as owning this place.'

'Too right,' said a new voice.

In the doorway stood a man in red coveralls. A number of insignia sewn to the chest made him look very grand, which was a contrast to the man himself, who looked not much older than Aaron. Both Joe Rivas and the Doctor were probably older than him.

He had short blond hair, blue eyes and a cheerful smile that made his eyes sparkle as if they were permanently watery.

'Hi there, everyone,' he replied. 'I'm Godfried.' He had a very slight accent that Sam tried to place. European definitely. German, or maybe Dutch?

The Rivas twins were walking towards him, hands outstretched ready to shake, with an eagerness Sam hadn't seen from them before.

'Mr Christoffel,' Jo Rivas said. 'A pleasure. I'm Jo. This is Joe.'

The newcomer nodded. 'Ah, yes, we spoke over webchat,' he said. 'Thank you for bringing the children to Moonbase Laika. I hope the trip was easy.'

'World State craft are always comfortable,' Joe Rivas said, like it was something he'd learnt to say in these situations. 'It's what makes World State so popular with travellers.'

Godfried Christoffel paused before answering. 'Of course,' he finally said.

'And now we are anxious to head back to Earth as soon as possible,' said Jo.

The surprise from the other visitors and even the Doctor was expressed vocally, loudly and all at once.

'Okay, okay, okay.' Joe finally quietened everyone down. 'We were never going to stay up here with you. World State got you here and we'll send another shuttle in three days to collect you. Our job is done.' He smiled as if that was the best news he'd ever heard. 'After all, you are perfectly safe here, in a World State Moonbase, with Mr Christoffel's crew. He's Chief of Security, you see.'

'Why do you need security on a Moonbase?' asked Michael.

Jo Rivas smiled at Christoffel. 'This is Michael. He asks a lot of questions.'

'Good ones,' the Doctor observed.

'And that's the Doctor. But presumably you've met.'

Christoffel looked at the Doctor. 'No.'

'Of course we haven't.' The Doctor stood up and walked over to him, flashing his strange little pass. 'Ministry of Moons and Moonbases. The Doctor. Hello.' He winked at Christoffel. 'And now we have. Met, that is. Marvellous.' He wandered back to where he had been sitting and put his feet up on a chair. 'Great Moonbase by the way. I'll be giving the canteen ten out of ten in my report, no problems.'

'Ministry of what?' asked the Chief of Security. 'I have never heard of it.'

'Course you haven't,' the Doctor said. 'Be a bit silly if you had – we could hardly do surprise inspections of all the Moonbases if you knew we existed, and were visiting.'

'We are the *only* Moonbase. Anywhere. Why is there a ministry of them?'

'Brand new,' the Doctor carried on. 'Only launched last month. Do you like that? Launched – like a space rocket. Deliberate choice of words, you see, all to do with the PR. I'm sure the Rivas twins here can tell you how important good PR is. And branding. And franchising. And . . . anyway, I'm sure your commander will be expecting me. Probably told to keep it all hush-hush. Just ignore me, pretend I'm not here and everything will be fine.'

Godfried Christoffel breathed out heavily and turned back to the Rivas twins. 'Anyway, I'm sorry, but no, you can't go.'

'What?'

'Of course we can!' Jo Rivas looked at her brother, as if he would magically change Christoffel's mind.

'It's the sunspots,' Christoffel explained. 'The course away from the Moon back home would need to be a different trajectory to avoid them but, because of the debris orbiting Earth and where the pockets of safe passage are through them, they're not aligned right now. You'll be here at least three days, so I've cancelled the other shuttle and you can all go home together after all.'

Sam took some pleasure in the obvious discomfort Jo Rivas felt at this news, although he wasn't sure why. Maybe it was because she had been so keen to dump them on the Moon and leave them here without actually telling anyone that had been the plan.

Her brother, however, was more upset than that. 'You don't understand, chief. We have to get away from here today.'

Christoffel shrugged. 'Sorry. Not going to happen.'

'Oh dear,' said the Doctor, with a wink at Sam and the others. 'Looks like we're all in this together. Shame World State didn't do something about all that space junk orbiting Earth beforehand, eh?'

'Space junk?' asked Caitlin.

The Doctor beamed at her. 'Over the last sixty-odd years, since humankind started sending satellites and spaceships and skylabs into space, the rockets that got them there have been abandoned, left to float in Earth's atmosphere. After so many missions, Earth is ringed by loads and loads of debris that hasn't burned up in the atmosphere yet. It's hazardous and wasteful. Funny thing is, your planet is finally starting to be more conscientious when it comes to recycling paper and stuff, but is still utterly pants at it up here in outer space. Wait another hundred years and you'll see you have the most awful reputation with the Galactic Federation as mucky puppies who don't clean up after themselves.'

'Galactic Federation?' asked Hsui.

Sam was more taken by the Doctor's 'your planet' comment, but before he could query it the Doctor was on his feet, arms round Aaron Relevy's shoulder, steering him out into the corridor and towards the portholes. The others slowly followed.

'See that, Aaron?'

'Yup. That's Earth.'

'Beautiful, isn't it?'

'Stunning,' said Hsui, and Sam noticed she was standing as close to Aaron as possible. 'Isn't it stunning?'

'Oh yes,' said the Doctor. 'But it's ringed by all this awful rubbish that you can't see from here. It's dangerous and will end up needing to be cleared or you'll find yourselves unable to go back and forth to the Moon, Mars or wherever you want to go without crashing into old *Soyuz, Apollo* or *Guinevere One* bric-a-brac. Now, you could do yourself a lot of good by setting up a nice programme to be watched by billions of kids all over Earth that tells them how important it is to keep space tidy. Maybe those that grow up to be scientists and mission controllers and astronauts will stop making such a garbage patch of your atmosphere.'

'Explorers in space,' Hsui said. 'We should be proud of everyone who has ever set foot up here.'

Aaron smiled at her. 'Absolutely.'

The Doctor paused for a second, then grinned at them both. Then he patted them both on the back, and somehow, as he turned away, he managed to link their arms around each other's waists.

'I do so love international romance,' he whispered quietly, so only Sam and Caitlin could hear.

'Anyway,' Joe Rivas said, 'that has nothing to do with World State and –'

'Nothing to do with World State?' echoed the Doctor, standing in front of Joe, towering over him slightly and fiddling with his bow tie. 'It has everything to do with World State. You people should be leading the charge, not ignoring it. That, Joseph Rivas, is why the ministry sent me. To check up on you, and your World State's attitude to such things. And, I have to say, I think my ministry is going to be very disappointed in you.' He threw a look at Jo. 'Both of you.'

Joe swallowed hard and opened his mouth to speak but all that came out was a high-pitched squeak.

Jo stepped in and smiled at the Doctor. 'Of course, you're right, we apologise.' Then she steered her brother back to a seat in the mess.

Christoffel gave the Doctor a look that suggested he enjoyed seeing the Rivases taken down a peg or two. 'Doctor, I'm glad the ministry sent you up. I apologise that somewhere along the way communications got scrambled and we were unaware you would be here, but I am delighted you are. It'll be a pleasure to have you see how well we have adapted the old base from its original use to what we have today.'

'What was it used for originally?' asked Hsui.

'I know,' said Michael proudly.

Christoffel smiled at him. 'Go ahead, Michael. What do you think it was?'

Michael seemed to grow an inch or two as he answered, pleased to be asked for his knowledge rather than having to force it on people as usual.

'This base was set up in 2006 by the Unified Intelligence Taskforce as a tracking station, keeping an eye not just on Earth but out into space – a sort of early-warning system in case of alien invasion.'

Joe Rivas was back beside them in an instant, eager to spin a bit of PR. 'Almost right. It was more of a scientific research station, exploring new ways to harness solar power, gravitational power and possible mineral sources to replace those we were running out of down on Earth – no one wants to run out of oil before we have a substitute. Then, in 2023, UNIT passed it over to World State, because private enterprise could fund the research even better. And that is us. Now, thanks to all of you, this base will stop looking quite so militaristic and more . . . comfortable and friendly. The people who work here were all very excited by your murals.' Joe looked at Christoffel. 'Maybe it's time to meet the staff?'

For some reason everyone turned to the Doctor, as if asking his permission.

He, however, stood there, tapping away on a device slightly larger than a smartphone.

Christoffel put his hand in his pocket and then reached out and took the device away from the Doctor.

'Mine, I think,' he said, half cross and half bemused. When exactly had the Doctor managed to take it out of his pocket without him noticing?

'Interesting stuff,' the Doctor smiled.

'What is?' asked Christoffel.

'Oh, you know what I mean.' He gently poked Christoffel in the chest. 'We need some answers, don't we, chief?'

The Doctor turned on his heel, hands wiggling above his head. 'This way, I believe,' he said, and walked on.

Shaking his head, Christoffel suggested they all follow him and prepare to meet the commander of Moonbase Laika. He started off at a bit of a pace.

Sam and Caitlin found themselves alongside the Doctor as he walked. He was looking around at walls, doors, windows, signs and anything else, muttering quietly and sometimes nodding.

After a few moments, Sam realised the Doctor was addressing the two of them, but quietly. 'You seem like intelligent children. For humans. Oh, you don't mind being called children, do you? I'm never sure I get that right – at what point you stop wanting to be called children, kids, offspring, *die kinder, les enfants* –'

Sam could imagine this going on for a while so he butted in. 'No, children is fine,' he said quietly. 'What did you find out from the chief's tablet?'

The Doctor tapped the side of his nose. 'Things.'

'Like about the vents?' asked Sam.

'I like the way you think, Sam. Yes, possibly. Apparently people have been disappearing.'

Caitlin gasped.

'Oh, don't worry,' the Doctor carried on. 'They come back, but with gaps in their memories. Just a few hours here and there. Random people, no obvious connection, no links.'

'Other than the fact they work here,' said Sam.

'Well, they'd have to,' said Caitlin. 'There's no one else here except the Moonbase Laika staff.'

'And us,' the Doctor corrected.

'And . . . maybe someone else?' offered up Sam.

'Maybe,' the Doctor agreed. 'But let's not worry about it.' He threw his arms round their shoulders as they walked. 'So, intelligent little offspring of humans, whose explanation for why this base was built did you prefer? Michael's or Mr Rivas's?'

'Perhaps they were both right?' suggested Caitlin.

'Oh. Oh, that's very good. Very observant. Well done.' He smiled at Caitlin, then turned to Sam.

'I agree,' Sam said. 'They might both be accurate. But I think Michael's explanation was more interesting.'

'Oh, it was,' said the Doctor. 'And your World State Brand Team Franchise-holding PR Gurus over there were a little too quick to give us the approved spiel. Because there's one other thing I want to know about this base that no one has mentioned.'

'What's that?' asked Caitlin.

'Why did UNIT give it up?' The Doctor looked up at the ceiling. 'I mean, they built it, funded it, and used it for a long time. I'm very surprised that they handed it over, unless World State offered them a lot of money.'

'World State does have a lot of money,' said Michael, joining them. 'Couldn't help overhearing.'

'So the question remains,' the Doctor carried on. 'Why? Why did UNIT sell it and why did World State buy it from them?'

Sam took a deep breath. 'Maybe UNIT didn't like the space snakes.'

'Possibly,' the Doctor said. 'Very possibly.'

Caitlin looked horrified and Michael snorted. 'Space snakes? What space snakes?'

'I have no idea at all,' the Doctor grinned. 'But if Sam here thinks it might be because of the space snakes, then we should find out if they really exist.'

'He's just made them up,' Caitlin said.

'Have you just made them up?' the Doctor asked.

Sam shook his head and quickly told them about the old man at the *BPXtra* studio and his warning.

'See?' said the Doctor. 'Sounds like space snakes to me.'

'He might have been ill,' said Savannah.

'Or drunk,' added Caitlin.

'Or lying.' That was Michael's contribution.

The Doctor nodded. 'He might also have been giving Sam here a warning for a very good reason. Best not ignore it, just in case. Let's see what the commander of this base has to say about space snakes when we get there.'

'And if he doesn't believe us?'

The Doctor shrugged. 'Then we'll ask about space cats, space bears, space badgers and even space alpacas. I'll wear him down – I'm good at that.'

'Okay, everyone,' Godfried Christoffel called back. 'You are now entering the main control area. Please do not touch anything.'

Sam gave the Doctor a look.

'What?' the Doctor said.

Caitlin gave him a similar look.

'You have only known me five minutes!' the Doctor protested. 'Why do you think that applies to *me* any more than *you*?'

Michael too gave him the look.

'Oh, all right,' sulked the Doctor, shoving his hands into his trouser pockets. 'Happy now?'

Christoffel turned the wheel on the door and swung it outwards, and everyone peered into the Command Area.

It was a circular room, with a couple of doors on the far side, opposite where they stood now.

Seated at a series of individual desks were men and women staring at touchscreen surfaces that lit up as they worked, reflecting a variety of colours and images on to their faces. Each of them wore coveralls in reds, blues and yellows.

On the right-hand side, the wall was one massive window, giving a fantastic view of the surface of the Moon. Earth could be seen floating in the pitch blackness of the starless sky. Sam stared at the vista.

'Wow,' he said. 'Just . . . wow.'

At which point a tall, dark woman in green coveralls stood up from behind a desk with lots of touchscreen controls on it.

'Good afternoon, everyone,' she said with a deep American accent that made Sam think of a country-and-western singer. 'Welcome to Moonbase Laika. My name is Morrison Cann. I'm the commander and, unless you listen very carefully to what I have to say, every single one of you will be dead before nightfall.'

Then she smiled at them.

# Chapter 8

# Spaceface

Sam looked around him, and nearly everyone looked the same: mouths hanging open, surprise or fear in their eyes.

*Oh good*, he thought. At least it wasn't just him.

Everyone except for Michael, that is. The brainbox of the gang didn't seem worried, and nor did the Doctor. Well, if the Doctor wasn't frightened, there was no need for Sam to be.

He took a deep breath and exhaled. Then he smiled at Savannah. This seemed to help her relax a bit too. Sam found he was smiling a bit more.

'Okaaaay,' said Joe Rivas. 'I'm sure Commander Cann is joking.'

'Absolutely not,' the commander replied in a firm, matter-of-fact voice. 'And, now that I have your attention, let me explain what I mean.' She tapped a finger on a wall and a touchscreen glowed into life. On it was a circular diagram that Sam recognised as a geometric map of Moonbase Laika.

'Moonbase Laika,' Cann continued, 'is a working station. And we expend a great deal of energy up here keeping the lights, life support, hydroponics, et cetera, all going. It's how we stay alive on a day-to-day basis. But to achieve that we must have strict energy-saving routines.' She tapped a number of the squares that Sam took to represent rooms on the map. They immediately went red. 'These areas are out of bounds after 9 p.m. CET in order to preserve what we need. Any areas marked in red are what we call dead zones. At night, when the base is manned by a skeleton staff, we shut down life support in these dead zones. There's no admittance to them. Don't try. Don't think it's a challenge or a game. It's not. These areas have Hardinger seals on them, but even so accidents do happen. If that accident involves you, I won't be writing a letter to your parents expressing my sadness at your instantaneous death. I'll be writing to say how stupid you were and deserved it because you didn't listen.'

'Seems harsh,' said Jo Rivas.

'It is harsh, Miss Rivas, because life on the Moon is harsh. In this place the slightest change in routine can kill. The base is set up to support a certain number of staff. Every time we have visitors, we have to adjust the artificial oxygen supply, the gravity, the food rations, everything. We can't just pop down to the nearest 7-Eleven for supplies, you know.' She looked at them all in turn. Sam felt her eyes burning into him, almost challenging him to defy her; he had no intention of doing so. 'You think I'm being harsh? That's nothing to what happens if you die here. I might tell your parents that your death was instantaneous – but it wouldn't be. It'd be painful. It would take you about three minutes to go unconscious but, before you did so, your eyes, ears and skin would rupture and you would be in agony. Only then would you die.'

She reached over to a tall red-haired man in red coveralls like Christoffel's, who was tapping some numbers into a touchscreen at a console. 'Lew?'

The man passed her a pile of papers, barely giving Sam's group a glance as he did so, then he returned to whatever he was doing.

The commander passed the papers to the Rivas twins. 'Distribute these to your party, please. It's a print-out of dos and don'ts. A list of which rooms everyone is sleeping in, as well as places of interest to go, places of danger to avoid. Again, I repeat: this is not a challenge. I'm glad you guys are here, and as one of the judges of the competition *BPXtra* ran I look forward to meeting you all individually and having a laugh. But, right now, it's important you understand exactly how dangerous this place is before you find out how great it is too.'

Nervously, Joe Rivas passed the papers around. 'Take one, pass it on,' he said.

Sam read his. Sure enough, it was a copy of the map, with each room numbered, a list of things not to do and a list of places to go. The base seemed very simple, and each room was clearly marked. The one they were in at the moment was one, the last room on the list was thirty-seven.

There was one place on the wall map that wasn't duplicated on the paper version, though. Instead it was just marked by a series of criss-cross patterns and no number.

'Excuse me,' Sam asked tentatively.

Commander Cann stared at him, as if sizing him up. 'It's Sam, isn't it?' she finally said.

Sam was taken aback, as was everyone else. How did she know his name?

'I make it my job to read up on everyone World State sends to visit my base,' she said, clearly guessing the source of his confusion.

'Er, right,' he said. 'I just wondered what this room is.' He held the map up.

Cann again called to the red-haired man. He looked across at the group, over the top of his glasses, like a teacher trying to spot a troublemaker.

When he spoke, his voice bore no resemblance to his size and stature. He had a soft, almost inaudible Welsh accent.

'Hi there. I'm Llewellyn Hughes, the Chief of Science on Moonbase Laika. And the area this young man has asked about is HEART.' He reached out and tapped the wall and a screen appeared. 'This is HEART,' he continued. 'It's the nerve centre of the base, the computer control. Everything that exists here works because of HEART.'

'If it's a computer,' said Michael, 'shouldn't it be called BRAIN?'

Hughes shrugged. 'Brains stop, but the body keeps going. Hearts stop, that's it. Everything withers and dies. Without HEART, this base is dead. That's why no one goes near it. No one except me and my immediate staff. Kindly stay away from it.'

'Well,' said the Doctor, 'that's all very straightforward. What next?'

Commander Cann crossed to the big window. 'I'd like to show our talented group here where their murals are going to end up across the Moonbase.'

Now that she'd delivered her scary pep talk, Cann was all smiles. She began ushering everyone towards a door at the rear of the room.

Sam and Savannah hung back a bit, staying close to the Doctor; somehow, Sam felt like that was a good idea. He watched as Cann and the others disappeared into the corridor. There would be an opportunity to catch up later. Right now, he wanted to spend more time with the Doctor.

The Doctor turned to Chief Hughes.

'What if something happens to you, Chief Hughes? Who looks after HEART then?'

The Chief of Science just smiled at him. 'I make sure nothing ever does. But I appreciate your concern, Mr . . . ?'

'Doctor. With a "the".'

Hughes and a couple of other people in the room momentarily stopped what they were doing and looked at the Doctor. Aware that he was being stared at, the Doctor coughed slightly, fiddled with his shirt collar and shuffled the shoulders of his jacket.

'Anyway,' the Doctor continued, 'just, you know, be careful.' He ushered Savannah and Sam forward. 'Come along, young-adult people things, let's catch up with the others.'

As they passed Godfried Christoffel, the young Chief of Security tapped the Doctor's arm. 'Where are you from again?'

'Ministry of Moons and Moonbases,' said Sam automatically.

'Yes,' the Doctor agreed. 'Ministry of what-my-mate-Sam-said.' The Doctor beamed at Sam. 'See – mates. Told you.'

Sam grinned back.

Christoffel was less impressed. 'Why are you really here, Doctor? Moonbase Laika is a very safe and secure place.'

The Doctor regarded him carefully, then spun round, glancing at each and every person in the Command Area – about twelve people in total. Most were working away, but Hughes and the others who had caught his glance earlier were all watching the Doctor intently.

It was almost, Sam thought, as though a small group of them knew more about the Doctor than anyone had realised. Not that Sam was sure how, or knew exactly what worried them.

'What do you think can go wrong?' That was one of the others, a middle-aged woman in blue coveralls.

The Doctor seemed momentarily caught off-guard. Then he shrugged. 'We're in space, and against all that spaceness this is a very small building with, frankly, not much between us and out there. Plus, the whole thing is controlled by a computer system that can only be accessed by Chief Hughes, which, for some reason, UNIT was more than happy to flog off to the first multinational corporation to hit the BUY IT NOW button on eBay. I can already think of eighty-five different scenarios of varying levels of go-wrongness that make me want to be somewhere else entirely. Oh, and my mate Sam thinks there are space snakes here, too.'

'Snakes on a base?' laughed Hughes. 'There's no such thing as space snakes!'

The Doctor held out his hands and shrugged. 'Who knows? But I trust the instincts of a fourteen-year-old boy over your safety protocols any day.'

'Oh?' said a slightly put-out Christoffel. 'And why's that?'

The Doctor pointed behind them all.

Everyone – and by now absolutely everyone in the room was listening to the Doctor – followed the direction of his pointing finger.

The Doctor was pointing outside, through the big picture window that dominated the far wall.

There, on the dusty surface of the Moon, four shapes slithered towards the base, then reared up, heads flicking back, yellow eyes glinting malevolently.

'Ladies and gentlemen,' said the Doctor quietly, and without any trace of told-you-so in his voice. 'I think those count as space snakes, don't you?'

# Chapter 9
# See the Lights

'Welcome to the planetarium,' said Commander Cann proudly. She had led the reduced gang there after a short walk round the ring, saying she was taking them somewhere special.

'What about Sam and Savannah?' Caitlin had asked, but Commander Cann had said they'd be with them in a moment, although she also looked behind her and grunted in annoyance. 'Well, they *should* be. I'm sure Chief Llewellyn will hustle them along.'

The planetarium was a massive room with a domed ceiling that, according to the commander, slid open to reveal a screen on to which things could be projected. Apparently it was meant to be an astrophysics guide, so the teams on Moonbase Laika could see how the stars moved and changed over the years. It was able to project images from over five hundred years' worth of recorded scientific history to map the changes and help predict what might happen in the future.

Commander Cann told the kids that the crew also used it to show 3-D movies from Earth and it was therefore known as the Chill-out Area – this was where their murals would be painted after all. Caitlin was especially happy to hear this.

'But there are no walls,' Hsui said. 'The dome comes right down.'

Commander Cann nodded. 'That's right. So what's the only space to paint on?'

'The inside of the dome itself?' suggested Caitlin.

'Correct. So, when people come in here to relax, to chill out, the entire room, everything they can see, will be covered by your beautiful designs,' the commander said. 'Except for when the dome opens to reveal the projector screen – and it'll all be in the dark then anyway – your paintings will amuse and delight everyone who comes here.'

'Wow,' breathed Caitlin. 'That is *so* cool.'

Michael nodded excitedly. 'It is.'

'Want to see something even cooler?' asked the commander. She produced a small remote from a pocket and aimed it at the ceiling, clicking on it as she did so. The inner dome split and started to descend, revealing the massive screen beneath.

A second click and, as the lights dimmed, a hologram of the solar system appeared on the screen.

'Okay,' said Aaron, nudging Hsui gently. 'Now even I think that's cool.'

Jo Rivas was still standing by the door, frowning.

'Everything okay?' her brother asked quietly.

'Can you hear that?' she said.

He listened. 'Nope, what?'

'I thought I could hear a noise.' She crouched down, her hand near the grille of an air vent at the base of the door where it met the floor. 'In here.'

Her brother shrugged. 'Probably just machinery. It's an air vent. Air vents probably pump air. Stop worrying about nothing. I'm more concerned that we can't go home yet and will be stuck up here for days. We do have other projects to work on, you know. More important ones than playing nanny to a bunch of geeky kids –'

Jo stopped him. 'Oh, just look at it this way,' she said. 'How often do we get to stand on the Moon?'

'Well, yeah, there is that,' Joe agreed. 'I mean, it is the Moon. That's kind of impressive.'

'Better than taking World State bigwigs around Scunthorpe!' Jo laughed, then stopped. 'There it is again. A hissing.'

She tried to wiggle her fingers through the grille but couldn't get them in. 'Can't feel any air leaking,' she said, relieved. Then she gasped.

'What's up?' her brother asked.

Jo pulled her hand back – the tip of one finger was bleeding slightly. 'Must have nicked it on something sharp,' she said, sucking her finger to get the blood off. 'Stupid Moonbase.'

Joe nudged her. 'Doesn't matter. We should probably focus on the commander. She might be telling the kids about hissing ventilation tubes.'

'Oh, very funny,' his sister said, taking her finger out of her mouth and shaking it.

'Hissss,' Joe joked.

The look he got in return suggested Jo Rivas wasn't finding her twin very funny at all.

Instead, she went back to listening to Commander Cann.

'Now then,' the commander was saying, pointing upward, 'what's that?'

'Mars,' Michael said.

'Good. So, if that's Mars and that's Earth and that's Venus, what's that?'

Caitlin turned to Michael, assuming he'd know, but he was silent, turning on his heel, counting the planets displayed above them. Then he did it again.

And again. 'That's impossible,' he muttered. 'And more than that, it's silly.'

'What's silly?' asked Aaron.

'We know all the planets and planetoids and dwarf planets and satellites and asteroid fields and . . . and that's silly.' Michael pointed up at a dull grey ball by Mars. 'That simply shouldn't be there.'

Commander Cann smiled. 'And yet, there it is.'

'Is it a test?' wondered Caitlin. 'To see if brainboxes like him know their stuff?'

Commander Cann shook her head. 'Nope, that's an extrapolation of how the solar system may have looked a few billion years ago. So can you tell me what that planet is?'

Michael shrugged. 'No idea.'

'None of the experts on Moonbase Laika have any idea either. It popped up some years back when the Hubble Space Telescope was trained on this area of space for a few days. We know this planet is very old and no longer exists. Like all things we see in space, it's actually sort of like time travel – because of the time it takes light to travel, we are actually seeing stars and moons and planets as they were thousands of years ago.'

Michael was so excited. 'Are you saying that Moonbase Laika's mission is to identify and catalogue that new planet? Or I suppose we should say that very old one?'

'Yes, that's one of the things we are doing here.'

Michael was almost beside himself. 'But why now? Why has no one seen it before? Oh wait, perhaps it's on a weird orbit. If it was in almost perfect alignment with Mars and significantly smaller, and our rotations matched it, it would nearly always be invisible to our telescopes because Mars would be in the way. Maybe it exploded!'

'Why would it do that?' asked Hsui.

'Planets do sometimes, especially if they have molten or ice volcanoes at their core. Maybe it disintegrated millions of years ago. This Moon, the moons of Mars and maybe some of the asteroid belt could be the remnants of it.'

For Hsui and presumably all the others this was way beyond them, but they were enjoying Michael's excitement, and finding it infectious.

Commander Cann was nodding, encouraging him, and clearly enjoying swapping thoughts with Michael, challenging him to think.

'Yes, good theory,' she said. 'That is what we are trying to establish. Did the Hubble get a reflection of the past, a unique snapshot of something that universal gravity had kept out of sight for centuries?'

'That's . . . that's brilliant,' Michael said. 'And exciting. And I want to come and live here and work here and find out!'

Commander Cann grinned. 'And hopefully when you are older you will, Michael. Because I seriously doubt we'll know the answers in the next decade or so, but hopefully we might in your lifetime. Maybe we'll find some more mysteries and questions at the same time. It would be boring if we knew everything now. Science is a slow but fantastic art.'

'Where are the others?' asked Caitlin, looking around.

'Other what?' Cann frowned at her. 'There aren't any other planets yet.'

'No. The Rivas twins,' she explained.

Everyone looked around the planetarium, but the brand team was nowhere to be seen.

'Stay here a sec,' Commander Cann sighed, bringing the lights back up as the dome closed over the screen. 'I'll pop out and find them.' She smiled at the group. 'You see, kids are as good as gold. Pesky adults can't be left alone for one minute.'

At which moment the loudest, most annoying alarm sounded throughout the base. Commander Cann started for the door, then turned back to the children. 'Aaron, you're oldest, you're in charge. No one leaves this room till I or one of the chiefs come back, okay?'

Aaron nodded. 'Okay.'

And she was gone.

They all stood staring at one another.

'I wonder what that alarm is for?' Michael said, voicing what they were all thinking.

'Nothing good,' Hsui said, moving closer to where the Rivas twins had been standing. 'Alarms never are.'

She was suddenly aware of a strange noise at her feet, down behind the grille – a sort of hissing.

# Chapter 10

# Repulsion

The alarms had sounded because Godfried Christoffel had hit a huge red screen on the wall by the window. A shutter had then closed down over the glass (or whatever glass-substitute it was), blocking everyone's view of the space snakes.

All over the room – and, Sam assumed, all over the Moonbase – shutters had come down.

'Emergency protocol Uniform November India Tango,' Godfried shouted and everyone in the room stopped what they were doing and went to different stations.

The lighting in the room dropped to a dull red and it took a few seconds for Sam's eyes to adjust. Once his eyes had got used to the red light, he realised the Doctor was at the centre of everything, calmly issuing

orders, and getting people motivated. Sam and
Savannah hung back, not wanting to get in the way.

After a few moments the alarm stopped and
Christoffel looked around the room. 'All stations
secured. General quarters established. Moonbase
Laika is secure and locked down.' From the doorway
came Commander Cann's voice, cutting across the
room, her tone daring anyone to be anything less than
on the ball. She'd obviously hurried back from
wherever she had left the others.

'I'm so glad,' she said. 'Now, who wants to tell
me why?'

As one, everyone in the room turned expectantly
to the Doctor.

'Oh,' he said. 'Oh, you think *I* know? Sorry, no,
not really. I mean, other than the big space snakes out
on the surface of the Moon, I'm not sure what the fuss
is about.'

'Space snakes?'

'It's true, commander,' said Llewellyn Hughes.
'We all saw them.'

'On the surface? The airless surface where nothing
can survive?'

'That's right,' said the Doctor. 'Well, except for
the bits that aren't right. Which would be the "where
nothing can survive" line, because clearly something

can.' He grinned at her. 'Be nice to know how, wouldn't it?'

'It would indeed,' Cann said. 'Godfried?'

The Chief of Security shrugged. 'Never seen anything like them, commander.'

There was a general murmur of agreement from the rest of the operatives, as Cann scanned the room.

'Tell me about the man who warned you,' said the Doctor – it took Sam a moment to realise that the Doctor was talking to him. Slowly, he told the story of the man he had met at the drinks machine and what he'd said.

'Not much to go on,' said Cann. 'A mad old man and a young lad who may or may not be exaggerating.'

'I'm not exaggerating,' said Sam crossly.

'Nevertheless, we need to know what those things are and why they are here now,' said Hughes.

'Oh, they've been here a while, I think,' the Doctor said.

'What makes you say that?' asked Cann.

'Well, Sam's old man for starters. And his red box. He said they'd been here before and that would suggest to me that he's probably someone who used to work on this Moonbase,' said the Doctor. 'What do we know about why UNIT built this base?'

'Research into deep space, warning and satellite guidance,' said the middle-aged woman Sam had noticed earlier. 'Pauline Brown,' she added, introducing herself. 'Medical Station Grade Three.'

'Thank you, Pauline,' the Doctor smiled. 'Good summation. Utterly wrong, but right I suppose if you believe the hype.'

'I'm sorry?' Cann strode towards him. 'Lew, can we have the lights back up?'

Immediately the red lighting gave way to the normal lighting, which seemed to make everyone relax a bit.

'Still on alert,' Christoffel crisply reminded the team. 'There's a bunch of space snakes outside.'

'Why aren't they trying harder to get in?' Hughes asked.

The Doctor shrugged. 'Oh, I imagine they can come and go as they please. Right now, they're just letting us know they are there. Watching. And waiting.'

'For what?' asked Cann.

The Doctor shrugged. 'No idea. But I reckon if they wanted to get into this base they wouldn't have much trouble.'

'What do you mean?' Cann was astonished. 'This place is literally airtight. Everyone that comes in or out is recorded. Every change of air pressure, every extra bit of water drunk is noted. No one can just walk through the airlocks and get in here.'

The Doctor threw an arm round Sam and Savannah's shoulders. 'What do you two think? What's the commander missing in all this?'

Sam looked at Savannah, who shrugged, but then her face lit up. 'They're snakes,' she said.

Sam got it too. 'They don't need to use the doors. They're small and thin.'

Commander Cann still couldn't grasp it. 'What do you mean? There's no other way in.'

The Doctor pointed to the floor. To a grille over the air vents that dotted the room. And every other room and corridor on Moonbase Laika.

'Your air vents are connected by what? Tiny, thin tunnels, pumping recycled air around on regulated timetables? So, in those downtimes you mentioned earlier, in those areas humans don't go into at night, I imagine that something which can live out there, on the surface of the Moon, and burrow beneath it, isn't going to be stopped by a few plastic tubes.' The Doctor turned to Christoffel. 'I'm guessing that over the last few weeks you've noted some unexpected pressure drops, just for a few seconds at a time? Too brief to register as people, and so probably ignored, put down to a fault in HEART's systems. But now we know what they were: our little silver friends out there, coming and going.'

Cann stared at Christoffel. 'Chief?'

He shrugged. 'Yeah, tiny drops, just a second here or there. Of course we never gave it much thought. Initially we suspected it was a steady leak, but we thoroughly checked that out – there was nothing.'

Commander Cann frowned and pointed at Sam and Savannah as she spoke to Christoffel. 'You didn't tell me? Didn't you think we should cancel these guys coming here if the base wasn't one hundred and one per cent safe?'

'I bet he did. He's a good Chief of Security.' The Doctor smiled. 'I bet that's exactly what you did. Rather than worry the commander over something so trivial, I bet you mentioned it to someone in engineering design at World State and got them to check the schematics first. Am I right?'

'Yes, I did. Word came back that World State thought it would be bad PR to cancel.'

'Really? I wonder why. Ah! Of course, I should have realised earlier. Aaron Relevy – he has a camera mounted on his baseball cap.' He turned to Sam and Savannah. 'Permanently recording everything?'

Sam reckoned so. 'Probably sends a feed back to Earth, too.'

'Unless the snakes want to be seen,' the Doctor murmured to himself. 'I wonder if they're receiving now . . .' He let all this sink in. 'They are clever and cunning. There's a lot of intelligence in those snakes. They want to be seen. Otherwise why say hello just now?'

'I don't understand,' said Savannah.

'Of course you don't,' smiled the Doctor. 'Why should you? At your age you should be thinking about exams and pop music and going on dates.' He stopped and looked at Sam. 'Well, she should!' he carried on. 'No, Savannah, you shouldn't have to worry that when UNIT was set up back in the 1970s it needed places to store things that it found – strange, alien things that it won in battle. Over the years they stored stuff in a variety of places – vaults, forges, Torchwoods even. But, at the turn of the century, they built themselves a nice little Moonbase up here, not to keep a safe eye on Earth – although I'm sure it helped – but as somewhere safe to store stuff. Space viruses, plastic-eating nanites from Phophov IV – oh, that was a battle and a half, believe me – plus guns, tanks and other assorted weapons too dangerous to leave on Earth. Then there's a Hopkiss Diamond. I had such fun vibrating that to communicate with its owners back on Jool. On their planet, Doctor translated as jeweller – Jeweller to the Stars, they named me. I like that. So much less aggressive than the Oncoming Storm, or Destroyer of Worlds, or Bow Tie of Doom. No one has ever really called me that, by the way. Bow ties are never doom-y. Well, rarely.'

The Doctor spun round and looked straight at Sam and Savannah. 'Oh, oh! I wonder if the RavnoPortal Beast of Birodonne is still locked away here. Now you'd love to see him. All he ever wanted to do was eat up little – No, no, perhaps you don't want to meet him, actually. Bad move. Bad RavnoPortal Beast of Birodonne. Baaaad.'

He addressed the commander again. 'So, that's the question. What happened to everything UNIT used to have up here, before World State so mysteriously bought this place? Did they take it somewhere else, or did they leave it here? Did World State inherit a nice empty Moonbase, or did it come with a literal arsenal of lethal lethalness? And, if so, why? We're a few decades off war, the Oil Apocalypse and the intellectual copyright battle between T-Mat and iTeleport. Lots of questions and no answers.'

'UNIT took everything as far as we know,' Christoffel said. 'World State inherited nothing.'

'Well, except for our serpent chums,' said the Doctor. And then suddenly he held up a hand. 'Shhhh. Listen.'

Everyone did so.

They could hear a tiny scrabbling sound, a faint hissing.

The Doctor pointed to one of the vents. Then another. And another.

'We have visitors,' he said. 'I'm not so sure we should invite them in, though.'

# Chapter 11

# Monster

Back in the planetarium, Hsui told Aaron about the hissing she'd heard from below.

'Machinery?' she wondered.

'The projection equipment?' he suggested.

'A leak? Are we losing air?' Michael said, earning himself a thump on the arm from Caitlin.

They had been warned about this more than anything in their training back on Earth. Of all the trials and tribulations that people living on Moonbase Laika faced, the ever-present threat of decompression was the most important to be aware of. Even the smallest hole, smaller than a pinprick, could kill everyone in seconds.

'We are *not* losing air,' Caitlin said.

'Well, actually –' started Michael, until Caitlin cut him off again.

'We. Are. Not. Losing. Air. All right?' she said, in a manner that dared Michael to argue.

He didn't.

It was then that they heard more sounds – slithering and sliding noises, which definitely seemed to come from beneath them.

Aaron took charge. He remembered what they had been told during an emergency drill situation when training for this trip.

'Sit down,' said Aaron. 'Like they taught us, in a circle.'

They all did as he said.

'Is everyone okay?' Aaron asked.

One by one they answered that they were okay, if a bit nervous.

'We stay here as long as possible, just like the commander asked,' Aaron said. 'We don't leave the planetarium until someone comes back to find us. Or unless we really need to. Basically, if something has gone wrong, this may be the safest place to be.'

'What makes you say that?' Hsui asked.

'Because we're not dead yet,' Aaron replied grimly.

Suddenly there was a massive hissing from beneath them, and everyone cried out in surprise as all the vent grilles – about six of them – flew away from the walls, as though some sort of massive pressure had been pushed against them.

'Everyone, get closer. Take someone's hand,' Aaron ordered.

'I'm not holding Caitlin's hand,' yelled Michael.

'You are now,' Caitlin replied. 'Grow up!'

Aaron grabbed Hsui's hand and squeezed it tightly. 'Form a chain,' he shouted. 'We are stronger and safer if we are one.'

'Not necessarily,' Michael muttered. 'If the place has sprung a leak, we'll all get dragged out into space together if we're holding hands.'

'Not helping,' Aaron said.

'Just saying.'

Suddenly the room was filled with flashes of silver.

Hsui screamed and Michael yelled.

*Snakes!*

The floor was swarming with slithering silver snakes, dashing about, rearing up and hissing at them.

Aaron's camera on his cap recorded it all: the snakes rearing up, spreading their hoods, dark yellow eyes glinting; the yells and cries of the gang, Aaron trying to keep them together so as to protect each other; and slowly trying to find a way towards the door. Aaron led the gang bravely, but with each turn they took, more snakes blocked their path.

After a few minutes, Aaron told them to stand still.

'They aren't attacking us!' he shouted.

'Yet,' Michael added.

But Caitlin could see what Aaron meant. 'They had a chance to, but they're not. They're just . . .'

'Herding us,' Aaron said slowly, realising that they were now standing right at the centre of the room.

The snakes stopped moving but never took their eyes off the gang.

'Why?' asked Hsui. 'Why don't they attack?'

Michael took a deep breath, trying to push down his fear and start thinking rationally, like the scientist that Commander Cann had suggested he might be one day.

'They want something,' he said. 'But not from us.'

'They are waiting,' Aaron agreed.

The planetarium door swung open and Godfried Christoffel rushed in with some of his men. In their hands they clutched fire extinguishers, which they activated, spraying the snakes with $CO_2$ foam.

The snakes moved fast, but not towards any of the humans. They went back the way they had come, disappearing into the vent tubes that lined the underside of the Moonbase.

Immediately everyone leapt forward with questions, but Christoffel shushed them. 'Let's get you back to the others,' he said and his men led the shaken but no longer scared gang away.

'Whose idea was it to stick together, to holding hands and form a chain?' Christoffel asked them as they headed out.

'Aaron's,' Hsui said proudly.

'Good call,' Christoffel said. 'Most people wouldn't think that quickly. Well done.'

Hsui was convinced Aaron grew a couple of inches with pride at that.

# Chapter 12

# Hunter and the Hunted

Christoffel led them into another room, a laboratory, called the Shaw Labs.

It smelt sterile and unwelcoming, but the gang was relieved to see Sam, Savannah and the Doctor there, setting out comfortable chairs and waving to each of them to sit.

Commander Cann was talking to the people who were there, most of whom were from the Command Area.

'Moonbase Laika is on lockdown. The crew have locked themselves either in their cabins or in the mess area. I have activated Emergency Code Alpha, so only the people with roaming privileges around the

Moonbase are the people in this room. That way
I know where everyone is. Moonbase Laika is
secure.'

'Apart from the space snakes,' said Hsui.

'They were all over the planetarium, commander,'
explained Christoffel. 'We fought them off, and they
went back into the vents.'

The commander blew air out of her cheeks.
'Doctor?'

'When they built Moonbase Laika,' the Doctor
said as he bustled around, 'they built it to withstand,
well, a lot. UNIT was good like that. Being
militaristic, they tended to make everything as
impregnable as possible.'

'Could a nuclear warhead take it out?' Sam
asked.

The Doctor gave him a look that suggested
probably not, but he didn't actually answer; instead
he waved an arm around the lab. 'This is the most
well-protected room other than HEART, according
to Chief Hughes. Which makes sense, because labs
on Moonbases are never the safest areas – all
those experiments and stuff that can go *boom!* at
inconvenient times. It's best to make sure nothing
external can get in and, in the event of chemical
fires or whatever, that nothing can get out.'

'And, yes,' Commander Cann added, 'just for the record, a nuclear warhead could destroy this place. So could the nuclear power core that makes it all work.'

Chief Hughes nodded. 'In the event of an emergency, from within HEART I can destroy –'

The Doctor put his fingers to his lips, making a shushing sound. 'I don't think our young artists need to know about that,' he said.

The Chief of Science nodded and sat down.

The Doctor smiled at all of them, visitors and staff alike. 'So, I imagine you're wondering why I've asked you here. Oh, I always wanted to say that. I sound like a proper academic.'

'Snakes?' suggested Michael.

'Indeed. Out there, on the surface, something is alive and "space snakes" seems to be a good description.'

'Scary metal ones.' That was Caitlin.

'Metal?' asked Savannah.

'Yeah, close up, it looked like they were made of metal,' Caitlin replied.

'So a potentially interesting life form, if you think about it.' The Doctor was up again, walking around. 'Reptilian life forms enhanced by some kind of living metal, maybe some kind of nanotechnology, maybe some kind of robot.'

'Or,' said Michael, 'snakes in spacesuits.'

Caitlin sniggered, despite her fear.

But the Doctor had stopped and was looking squarely at Michael. Then he glanced up to Hughes, Christoffel and the commander.

'That, young man, is brilliant.' The Doctor was now standing by Hughes. 'We simply didn't consider that – snakes in spacesuits. We need suits to live on or under the Moon's surface – why shouldn't they?'

'Because they are snakes?' Hughes suggested. 'Alien snakes. That have just swarmed through this base.'

'In spacesuits,' added Michael.

'Well, they've swarmed over one specific part of it: the planetarium,' said Aaron.

'Were they actually doing anything other than slithering around?' asked the Doctor.

Aaron shrugged. 'Probably. I wasn't really thinking about that.'

'No,' said the Doctor calmly, placing a hand on Aaron's shoulder. 'No, of course you weren't. You were saving everyone else's lives. Which is exactly what you should have done. Thank you.'

'What for?' Aaron asked.

'Being brave. And brilliant.' He swung back to the others. 'So, why swarm into the planetarium – the Chill-out Area, as I believe you call it? What's in there of all places? I mean, they can get through the vent tubes, which gives them access to everywhere on Moonbase Laika, so why go somewhere so insignificant? Command Area? No. These labs? No. Living quarters? Food halls? Nope, just the big, shiny recreation room.'

'Perhaps they wanted to watch a movie,' Caitlin said, remembering what Commander Cann had said before.

'Not likely,' the commander muttered.

'Or,' said Michael slowly, 'perhaps they wanted to see something else.'

Hsui clapped her hands. 'The planets, the stars. We were looking at those before the alarm started.'

'When we saw the snakes outside on the surface,' Savannah added.

'As a distraction,' Sam added. 'We were busy worrying about them, giving others time to get into the planetarium.'

'Absolutely,' the Doctor agreed. 'Clever snakes in spacesuits. Oh, I love you kids. You all think outside the box. Brilliant. You are all brilliant. Be more brilliant – why would they want to see the images of the solar system? I mean it's pretty and all that, but hardly unique.'

'What about that strange planet, the one we didn't know whether it was old or new?' Michael said to the commander.

'Oooh, what new old planet?' asked the Doctor, and Commander Cann repeated to him what she had told the others.

'And the Rivas twins?' asked Hsui.

'Oh, yes. Where are they?' The Doctor looked around the room as if he'd only just noticed they were missing. He even looked under a bench. 'Not really very likely, is it, Doctor,' he muttered to himself. 'You'd see them hiding under a bench. Think straight.'

'They wandered off, and I couldn't find them anywhere,' Commander Cann said. She turned to Christoffel. 'Chief, you'd better get some people out looking for them.'

The Doctor held a hand up. 'Hang on.' He looked at Christoffel. 'Is it true others have gone missing recently?'

Christoffel tried not to glance at his commander, but everyone noticed.

'I'll take that as a yes,' the Doctor said.

'Not exactly,' said the commander, with a sigh, then she muttered, 'This is so not my best day. Over the last couple of weeks, a number of staff have gone missing for a short space of time, but we always find them eventually, usually in their cabins. They have no memory of how they got there or of anything else.'

The Doctor turned to Pauline Brown. 'Pauline?'

She shrugged. 'Our best guess at first was some kind of electric shock, causing temporary amnesia. But we had no real answers.'

The Doctor smiled grimly at the commander. 'Amnesiac staff. Power losses. Space snakes in silver spacesuits. You're right, it's just not your day, is it?'

'Thank you,' the commander said. 'Anything useful to add?'

'When was the last case, Pauline?'

She glanced at Llewellyn Hughes. 'This morning, wasn't it – Sym?'

The chief nodded in agreement. 'One of my staff, doing routines in HEART, found himself in the mess shortly before you lot arrived.'

The commander suddenly looked at the Doctor.

'Oh, don't give me that "Oh, so it's all *your* fault" look, commander. That gets boring very quickly, with all the questions and the "Where were you when A happened to B". Trust me, it's got nothing to do with me.'

'Oh great,' the commander drawled. ' "Trust me", he says. Like I have any choice.'

'Can't the big computer help us?' the Doctor asked. 'See if it can find any links between the disappearances, the power losses and the arrival of the outer-space reptile race?'

Chief Hughes nodded. 'I'll go program the variables into HEART and see what it can suggest.'

'If HEART could scan under the Moon's surface,' Michael suggested, 'that might tell us where the space snakes are.'

'I like him,' the Doctor said. 'A lot. Chief?'

Hughes nodded. 'Worth a try,' he said, then looked at Michael. 'Want to come with me?'

Michael was standing beside him faster than the others could blink.

'Stay in contact, please,' the Doctor requested.

Christoffel opened a drawer, took out some headsets and tossed them to Hughes.

'Thanks,' Hughes said, fitting one to Michael and then the other to himself. 'We'll talk you through everything,' he said.

Christoffel activated a large widescreen monitor built into the wall and on to it appeared a split image of thin green lines, one above the other. 'Speak,' he said to Michael.

'What should I say – oh, cool!'

As he'd spoken, the green line on the screen became a waveform.

When Hughes spoke, the upper line did the same. 'It's two-way, Doctor. You just speak aloud and we can hear you.'

'Magic,' the Doctor said.

'Science,' said Michael, grinning at him.

'Get outta here,' the Doctor laughed. 'And, chief?'

'Doctor?'

'Be careful. Both of you. We've lost the Rivas twins. I don't want to lose you two as well.'

'We'll be fine.'

The chief and Michael left the lab.

The Doctor turned to Aaron. 'Mr Relevy?'

'Yes, Doctor?'

'You've been in show business a while, right? Tell me about that camera on your cap.'

'Records via bluetooth to a hard drive in my luggage. Broadcast-quality digital visual transmissions to Earth from up here are still a bit in the future.'

'So, my question is, is anything you see here being transmitted back to World State right now?'

'No.'

Sam looked at him. 'But I thought . . . ?'

'It's a fake, a lie,' Aaron said. 'Of sorts. I mean, the footage will end up on Earth and will be shown, but it's just being recorded and stored for now. I'm meant to upload a package each night and then transmit it back. Then they'll edit and broadcast.'

'But everyone on Earth thinks they're seeing real-time broadcasts.'

'Everyone knows there's a time delay. It's like the old *Big Brother* live feeds from twenty years ago – everyone knows it's not really live. But, in this case, the delay is more than a few moments. Just in case.'

'In case what?' asked Savannah.

'In case it all goes wrong,' said Sam quietly. 'And we all die.'

'Die?' said an alarmed Caitlin. 'They said everything was safe up here. World State never warned us about space snakes –'

'Well, good,' the Doctor cut across her. 'Your *BPXtra* is going to witness a peaceful encounter with charming space snakes in spacesuits.' He smiled. 'Back in the planetarium, I presume you got the whole thing on camera?'

Aaron nodded. 'I guess so, yeah – must've.'

The Doctor threw an arm round his shoulder. 'Never stop recording, Mr Relevy. It could be very important, historically speaking – it seems our clever old snakes want witnesses to the history being made up here.'

'Doctor?' Pauline indicated the readings
coming from the speaker sets worn by Hughes and
Michael.

'Can you hear us, Doctor?' asked Michael. The
green line wavered and changed in rhythm with
his voice.

'Absolutely, Michael. Where are you?'

'We're outside HEART,' Chief Hughes said.

'The chief is entering the access codes so we
can get in.' Michael sounded excited and the green
lines bounced up and down even more, as if to
underline this.

There were a few seconds of silence.

'Guys?' said Commander Cann. There was no
response.

'What's going on?' Sam asked, but the Doctor
hushed him.

More silence, although they could hear both
Hughes and Michael breathing; the effect on the
waveforms was slight but reassuring. Then the
waveforms fluctuated at the noise of a door opening,
a complicated-sounding series of clicks and whirrs as
lots of small parts opened one at a time.

Sam looked around the room at the various people
in coloured coveralls looking concerned, including
Pauline and Christoffel. They were the only Moonbase

staff not locked safely in their cabins, all being brave together during the emergency.

The Doctor stood completely still, eyes tightly closed, listening intently.

Caitlin had sat on her hands to stop herself fidgeting, clearly trying her best not to be scared.

And Savannah stared at the Doctor, as if hoping he would have all the answers.

Sam was convinced he already had them. He had faith in the mysterious Doctor.

Next to Hsui was Aaron, whose hand slipped casually into hers and gripped tightly. She gripped back.

Still nothing.

'Chief?' the Doctor said suddenly. 'Report?' His eyes snapped open.

Nothing.

'Lew?' Christoffel asked.

'Michael?' Savannah tried.

Nothing.

The waveforms were straight lines.

No sound. Not even breathing.

It was as if Michael and the Chief of Science had simply vanished.

# Chapter 13

# Bulletproof Heart

Realising that they had lost contact with Llewellyn Hughes and Michael Griffin, the Doctor and Godfried Christoffel came up with another plan.

It sounded equally insane, Sam reckoned.

'We'll go after them, retrace their steps,' said Christoffel.

'Um, no you won't,' said Commander Cann.

'Look, Plan A failed, and I'm feeling rather responsible for that,' the Doctor replied. 'And very responsible for Chief Hughes and young Michael. So Plan B it is.'

Christoffel argued. 'First we have to know –'

'We do know,' snapped the commander. 'Either the snakes didn't want them getting into HEART, or they've taken them over to do something specific – which implies that the snakes can't actually get into

HEART itself. Maybe the energy it gives off repels them.'

The Doctor was making a gesture with his arm, wriggling it, doing a pretending-to-be-a-snake thing, but in silence. Then he pointed straight up, into the ceiling, and made a mime that was about long tubes and tunnels and involved more arm wriggling.

Sam realised he meant that the snakes were inside the base, within the slender tubes that contained the power cables threaded throughout the ceilings and floors of the base. A perfect way to get around without being detected.

The Doctor put his hand to his ear and again did the arm-wriggling gesture. He meant the snakes had overheard their conversations!

Sam watched as the Doctor finished his mime. He slowed and stopped, as he and Sam both became aware that everyone in the lab had stopped watching the Doctor and were now looking behind him, to the doorway.

Standing there was a group of people.

Llewellyn Hughes. Michael Griffin. The Rivas twins.

'Hello,' said the Doctor. 'Love people who know how to make an entrance.'

'I want to go home,' said Michael.

'Well, obviously,' said the Doctor. 'But I'm not sure that right now we can —'

'I want to go home,' said Jo Rivas.

'Home is important,' said Joe Rivas.

'I'm sensing a theme,' said the Doctor.

'It couldn't be located,' said Hughes. 'Where is the red box?'

'They've been taken over by the space snakes!' said Caitlin.

'Haven't they just?' the Doctor murmured, wandering towards the newcomers. 'Bite marks on the hands, certainly.' He waved a hand in front of Hughes's face, but got no reaction. 'Hello?'

'We have to leave,' said Michael. 'Now. Go home.'

The Doctor stepped back. 'I think we got the message. May I ask a question?'

All of them said 'Yes' at the same time, their heads turning in unison, like puppets being controlled simultaneously.

The Doctor held out his hands. 'Are you responsible for the power losses? The crew getting amnesia?'

'Yes,' the four chorused in that same eerie way.

'Why?' Commander Cann asked.

'We were investigating your base,' replied Joe Rivas alone. 'We want the red box.'

The Doctor paused, just for a brief second, then burst into a jumble of hand-waving and walking in circles. 'Of course,' he said. 'Remember I said this used to be a UNIT base, full of weapons and alien artefacts and stuff? Well, the snakes are knocking on your door politely. Sort of politely anyway. Trying to ask for help.'

'Help?' said Commander Cann.

'Yup, commander. These are aliens, yeah? Aliens who want something UNIT took, something you, World State, whoever, inherited. "Can I have my ball back, please?" That sort of thing. Except "ball" could mean utterly lethal thermonuclear warhead, or huge vial of devastating bubonic outer-space plague, or perhaps even the massive RavnoPortal Beast of Birodonne.' The Doctor turned back to the mesmerised group. 'So, you don't want to hurt anyone, but you make people want to go home. That makes you rather antisocial space snakes in spacesuits. Tell you what, why don't you talk to me directly rather than through intermediaries. I get very bored talking to monkeys when the organ-grinder isn't far away. Don't want to talk to the handymen when the gaffer is . . . anyway, I think you get my point.'

He stood, waiting. Perhaps expecting a snake (but hopefully not a hundred) to flop out of the ceiling to have a chat.

It didn't happen.

'Well, that was an anticlimax,' the Doctor said.

He pushed past the possessed people and into the corridor. 'Plan B again, Mr Christoffel. Which way to HEART, please?'

The commander was with him in a second. 'Again, I don't think that's wise. I don't think I can afford to risk losing you too, Doctor.'

'Very flattering, yes and you're right, you probably can't afford to lose me because without me, no one's going to get through to the snakes, find out what's going on and free the minds of those four people.' He poked Commander Cann's shoulder. 'I'm pretty magnificent really and that's why I want to keep on the move. If I stay around here, they might start making more and more hostages out of you lot and I'll achieve nothing. This way, I may learn something useful with which to negotiate.'

Sam and Savannah had followed them to the door of the laboratory. 'Do you need anyone to come with you?'

The Doctor thought about this. 'Savannah, I want you two to see if you can help the commander find anything, anything in the records of this place that might help us work out what they want.'

'They want a box,' Aaron called out.

127

'Lot of boxes on a Moonbase like this,' the commander said.

'Any red ones?' Hsui wondered.

'We should also consider why they took the Rivas twins,' the Doctor said. 'What do they want with them?'

'Hostages?' suggested Christoffel.

The Doctor shook his head. 'Everything they've done has had a reason, nothing has been random.' He turned to Aaron and Hsui. 'World State, they represent World State. Maybe it's something to do with that. Can you remember either of them carrying any red World State boxes?'

'I don't think so,' Hsui said. 'I didn't see them with anything like that.'

'Their smartphones,' Aaron said, thinking aloud. 'They were always on them – if they have anything on any of us, I bet it'll be stored on their phones.'

'Password protected, I bet,' said Hsui. 'They seem the type to be security-minded.'

Aaron walked over to where the four people were standing, motionless. Almost as if they had been switched off.

Aaron reached into both Jo and Joe's pockets and took out their smartphones. 'Easy,' he said.

'Now what?' asked Hsui.

Aaron smiled. 'I'm a man who builds top-of-the-range tech from scrap metal. Getting past a few encrypted passwords should be a doddle,' he said. 'And those two are unlikely to use anything too complicated in case they need to access one another's phones in an emergency. Give me ten minutes with a computer on this base and I can sort it.'

'Good man,' said the Doctor. 'You do that. Caitlin, look after Michael and the others. Can you do that for me?'

Caitlin swallowed hard, then said, 'Of course, Doctor.'

'Thank you,' he said and winked at her. 'And Chief Christoffel?'

'Doctor?'

'The snakes are coming in through the vent grilles. Might be worth a round of blocking them up for now, just till we get this sorted?'

Christoffel sighed. 'And if we don't?'

'Then perhaps the snakes will have killed us long before we run out of clean air,' said Commander Cann.

'Oh, if the snakes wanted us dead,' the Doctor said, 'they could have smashed in the windows and sucked us all to our doom ages ago. No, I'm not getting hostility from them – they didn't hurt the guys in the planetarium or anyone they've knocked out. No, no, they need us alive and kicking.'

'Okay,' said Commander Cann. 'Heaven knows why, but I'm placing the safety of Moonbase Laika in your hands, Doctor. Don't get us all killed. Please.'

He smiled at her. 'I'll try not to.' He then nudged Sam. 'Well, Mr Miller?'

'Yes, Doctor?'

'Come with me?'

'Absolutely!' Sam grinned.

Together they wandered off down the corridor, talking all the time.

'Are you scared, Sam?'

'A little,' Sam confessed. 'But it seems kind of okay when you're around.'

The Doctor smiled. 'Glad to hear you say that. Now let's consider what we know. Snakes on a base. Searching for a box. Been everywhere they can. Can't find it.'

'Apparently they saw something in the planetarium,' offered Sam.

'True, true – but what? Should we pop in there, see if there's anywhere to hide a red box?'

Sam thought about it, then said no. 'The others were there and someone like Aaron would remember if there was a red box – he's quite sharp.'

'He is indeed,' the Doctor agreed. 'So let's forget the planetarium for now. Which brings us back to our current destination.'

'HEART?'

'HEART indeed. I think the commander is correct – the snakes keep taking over people who work in there, but they clearly can't go inside themselves. The energies it gives off can't be good for them.'

Sam was counting the facts off on his fingers. 'So if the red box is inside HEART, how come no one has ever seen it?'

The Doctor clapped his hands. 'Red box! Of course, *I've* seen the red box!'

'Where?' asked Sam.

'About ten years ago, out on the surface of the Moon. Lukas Minski – lovely man, bit preoccupied I reckon. I thought I saw something move but he dismissed it. But what if he encountered the snakes right then? What if it's *his* red toolbox we're looking for?'

Sam nodded, caught up in the Doctor's enthusiasm. 'So . . . so what's inside the box?' he asked.

'Not. A. Clue.' The Doctor stopped walking and closed his eyes, probably trying to picture what he saw several years ago, Sam reckoned. 'Nope, nothing. But I have something the snakes don't,' he added as he started walking again. 'My secret weapon, if you like.'

'A gun?'

'Okay, not a weapon. Bad choice of words. Infinitely better than anything as yukky as a gun.'

'What is it then?' Sam wondered.

But the Doctor just winked and said nothing else until they reached HEART.

The door was open, revealing the glowing interior, just as Hughes and Michael had left it when they were taken over by the space snakes.

Taking a deep breath, the Doctor walked in.

'Is it safe?' Sam asked.

'Unless you're an outer-space space snake, absolutely.' The Doctor waved him inside.

Sam looked around HEART. The walls glowed with a variety of different colours, as if HEART was alive, breathing. Beating silently.

It was warm. It smelt . . . odd.

'It's electrical.' The Doctor licked his finger and held it up. 'Supercharging the air. That's probably what can't be good for our reptile chums.'

'It's like just before a storm hits,' Sam said.

They looked around the HEART chamber. It was no larger than an average living room, but it was like a cylinder that rose up quite a long way. Sam couldn't actually see the top because the flashing lights made everything up there too hazy to focus on. 'Wow,' he said. 'This is amazing.'

A series of small ladders were fixed to the wall and, like Sym Sergei had done some hours earlier, the Doctor started climbing up into the heart of HEART.

'Everything on Moonbase Laika is controlled from here,' he called down to Sam. 'Everything. That's an incredible feat of engineering. And a bit stupid.'

'Why stupid?'

'Well obviously it's stupid. I mean, sabotage this place and you wipe out the base.'

'More proof the snakes want us alive then,' Sam said. 'If they took over the people that control this, like Chief Hughes, they could have killed us easily.'

'I like the way you think, Sam,' the Doctor said, waving his hand through the air. 'And now it's secret-weapon time.'

The Doctor produced something from his inside pocket. It looked like a big pen or thin torch, and it made a buzzing sound and glowed green as he ran it over a number of HEART's glowing panels.

'What is it?' Sam asked.

'Say hello to my sonic screwdriver,' the Doctor said. 'An app for every occasion. Except wood. And water. And it's not hot yet on deadlock seals. But a good old microstate seal like this – easy-peasy lemon squeezy.' Suddenly one of the panels stopped glowing and dropped forward. The Doctor reached inside, and then smiled. 'Gotcha. Oh, Lukas Minski, you clever man.'

He pulled out a red toolbox.

Sam grinned. 'How did you know where to find it?'

'Set the sonic to find an irregular energy pulse, because I guessed Lukas had hidden it where no one would look, and it was just blocking enough of the energy for the sonic to notice, but not enough for Moonbase Laika's less sophisticated instruments to detect.'

Sam was startled. ' "Less sophisticated"? But this place is state-of-the-art . . .'

The Doctor switched off his sonic screwdriver. 'And my little sonic here makes this Moonbase look like a prehistoric cave dwelling.' He patted one of HEART's panels. 'No disrespect intended.'

He jumped down and passed the red toolbox to Sam. 'Please can you take this? I may have my arms metaphorically full when we get back to the lab and chat to the snakes.'

'Why?' asked Sam.

The Doctor shrugged. 'Because they want it back.'

'So can't we give it to them?' asked Sam.

The Doctor paused. 'Maybe. Maybe not. I rather want to know what is in it before I give it back to them. They've not exactly been upfront about this, and there's a lot of biting been going on. I don't like bitey things as a rule.'

A new thought crossed Sam's mind, and he looked at the red box. 'It's not a bomb, is it?'

The Doctor stopped. 'Ooh. Ooh, I hadn't considered that. Maybe it is.'

Sam frowned. 'Great. I'm carrying a bomb.'

'Well, we better get it away from all this energy flying about in HEART then.' The Doctor strode off. 'Come along, Sam. Time to talk to the snakes.'

# Chapter 14

# Banging on the Door

Hsui, Caitlin and Savannah were grouped around Michael. The Rivas twins and Chief Hughes were stood slightly apart, but that was because they had moved as the trio gathered around their friend.

'Michael?' Caitlin said quietly. 'Michael, can you hear us?'

'I want to go home,' said Michael dully. He was just repeating it over and over again, as if it was the only thing he could say.

'We all do,' Savannah said.

And then it hit Caitlin – something the Doctor had said, about the whole "going home" thing.

'Got it!' she said rather loudly.

Everyone in the laboratory stopped whatever they were doing.

'What do you mean, Caitlin?' asked Commander Cann.

Caitlin took a breath. She didn't want to muck this up, in case no one took her seriously. She wondered how the Doctor would get this across to everyone. All these experienced people living on the Moon, living in space, and here she was, eleven years old and maybe about to solve a mystery.

Or make a fool of herself.

*Here goes nothing,* she thought.

'It's not Michael and the others who want to go home,' she started. 'The space snakes are talking through them, yes? So it's them. The snakes are telling us they want to go home.'

'Where is home?' the commander wondered.

'That planet,' said Caitlin. 'The mysterious one you and Michael were talking about earlier, in the planetarium. That's why they swarmed in there – they wanted us to see that planet, but we'd already switched it off.' Caitlin smiled. It made sense to her anyway.

Commander Cann grinned. 'You know what, guys, as theories go, I've not heard a better one.'

Caitlin almost blushed with pride. She'd been right to speak up.

'And you won't hear a better one . . .' said a voice from the laboratory door.

'Doctor!'

'Because Caitlin is utterly correct,' the Doctor finished, as he carefully closed the door behind him. 'Well, I've only heard about the planet, obviously. I haven't actually seen it, but it sounds plausible.'

Sam was holding the box out carefully. Old, red and metallic, like the strange old man had said.

'You found it?' Chief Christoffel said. 'What is it?'

'Hopefully not a bomb,' Sam muttered.

'You know what, I reckon it's just a box, Sam,' the Doctor said gently.

Sam wanted to feel convinced, but he wasn't entirely. 'That man I met on Earth mentioned this box to me. And he warned me about the snakes. Why did he tell *me*?'

'Wrong place, wrong time,' the Doctor said. 'Could have been any of you who saw that man, but it happened to be you, Sam. Tell us again what happened.'

'He walked over and warned me about the snakes, told me to look out for a red box and said goodbye.'

'Anything else?' prompted Commander Cann.

'We shook hands.' Sam remembered. 'Oh, and he said something weird as he left.'

'Yes?' the Doctor encouraged.

Sam frowned. 'I wasn't really listening at the time, but now it seems appropriate. He said something about it being time to go home.'

The Doctor nodded.

'But if the snakes want the box,' asked Caitlin, 'why didn't they get it themselves?'

Savannah laughed for the first time in ages. Sam thought it was a nice sound. 'They're snakes,' she said. 'No hands – how could they carry it from where Sam found it?'

She smiled at him proudly. Sam was about to say that, strictly speaking, the Doctor had found the box, but the Doctor nudged him. 'He was brilliant, Savannah. I'm very proud of him.'

Sam was delighted to see Savannah grin more broadly. And this time Sam didn't blush.

'Speaking of which – where was it?' asked Christoffel. 'I mean, I have no idea what's going on here, but it seems a reasonable question.'

'Inside HEART, locked away in a safe place all those years ago, where the power and energy in HEART would keep whatever is inside it safe, I imagine,' the Doctor said. 'And, because of the energies inside HEART, the snakes couldn't go in and get it themselves. That and, as Savannah said so brilliantly, how were they going to get it out anyway? They needed a human to do that.'

'So why you?' asked Caitlin.

'Oh, it's not really about me,' the Doctor smiled. 'But a few years back I was standing in a spacesuit, next to a man called Lukas Minski, when I saw him open this box. So I can at least remember the access code.'

'You were there?' asked Commander Cann. 'Then where is he now? He needs to explain why he put it in HEART.'

'He's on Earth,' said Sam. 'That's the man I saw, wasn't it, Doctor?'

Aaron was more concerned with the snakes. 'Okay, but why are they here? What do they want now?'

'Remember what I said earlier, Aaron? To Commander Cann over there, about aliens turning up and asking for their ball back? I think these guys want their metaphorical ball back – whatever it is, it's been locked inside a red metal toolbox for the past decade.'

'Are you sure they should have it?' asked Hsui.

Suddenly there was a terrible noise, like a massive hammering on the doors of the laboratory, and the walls, and the floors.

'Snakes,' said Christoffel.

'Space snakes in spacesuits,' added Savannah.

'Space snakes in spacesuits who would very much like to come in and get whatever's in the box, I reckon,' said the Doctor.

'Should we let them in?' asked Caitlin.

'Oh, yes,' said the Doctor. 'I think it's time we finished this little mystery once and for all.'

He crossed to the door, turned the handle and let the snakes in.

# Chapter 15

# Stars will Lead the Way

Godfried Christoffel and the rest of the Moonbase Laika staff, including even Pauline Brown, formed a protective circle round the children and the other visitors.

'They aren't going to hurt anyone,' the Doctor said loudly enough for everyone to hear. 'Because if they do, they'll annoy me. And that's their only bargaining chip gone. Unhappy Doctor means they don't get inside this box.'

Sam was astonished to see the snakes actually slither backwards slightly.

He stared at them in horrified fascination. He could see, now he was right up close to them and not running away, that they were indeed, just as Michael had suggested earlier, wearing silver spacesuits, clearly designed to survive in zero gravity, and transparent globes covered their cobra-like heads, some of which were open, presumably allowing the snakes' jaws to bite anyone if they felt the need. Other than that, they were the size of snakes on Earth, sleek, shiny and very hostile-looking. Their eyes glowed a fierce, luminous yellow and their heads swayed from side to side, as if sizing up their enemies.

Sam hoped they weren't getting ready to rip everyone's throats out.

The Doctor took the red toolbox from him and slowly turned to face the space snakes.

Sam heard him make some very strange noises, which seemed to come from deep within his throat. They weren't words; they were noises, breaths, staccato-style, but deep and quite scary. For a second, Sam wondered if the snakes had somehow taken him over too, but he seemed fine.

The snakes, however, backed even further away, except for one that came closer to the Doctor, reared up and spread its cobra-like hood even wider.

The leader, Sam guessed.

And then it made similar sounds back at the Doctor.

'Absolutely,' the Doctor said to the snake. 'And I'm afraid it hurts my throat to do it, so I'd prefer to speak English, if that's okay?'

The snake made another guttural hiss.

Sam and the others just stared at the Doctor.

'You speak Snake?' called Caitlin. 'Are you like Harry Potter?'

'No,' the Doctor said. 'But I do speak Outer-space Alien Snake. And I'm very different from Harry Potter – although I did get locked in a cupboard under the stairs when I was your age by my uncle.'

'Cool.'

'Not especially. But I had been very naughty and deserved it.'

'Doctor!' That was Commander Cann.

'Yes?'

'Space snakes? Danger? Mesmerised people?'

'Oh, yeah, sorry,' the Doctor shrugged. He offered the box to the leader snake. 'You want this, but there are terms.'

The leader snake hissed angrily.

'Fine. No talky nicely, no boxy-woxy.'

*Hiss.*

'That's better. Release everyone from your mental control. That's mean and unnecessary.'

Instantaneously Michael, the Rivas twins and
Chief Hughes staggered and all started talking at once,
asking what was going on, where they were, how they
had come to be there . . . and then they all yelled
'Snakes!' rather pointlessly.

'Shut up!' the Doctor ordered.

They did.

'Glad to have you all back,' he then said a bit more
kindly. 'Everyone okay?'

'I feel sick,' said Michael.

'To be expected,' the Doctor said. 'You'll be fine in
the morning.'

Commander Cann pushed her way through the
protective circle and joined the Doctor and Sam by
the leader snake.

'Look, sorry, but I demand to know what is going
on here on my base, Doctor.'

'I don't think it's really your base, commander.'

'Okay, World State's base.'

'Not what I meant. They see this as their base.
Been here longer than World State. Longer than
UNIT, and even the base being built, to be
honest. How many millions of years have you
waited?'

The leader snake hissed.

'That long? Wow.'

The Doctor took out his sonic screwdriver. He aimed it at the large widescreen monitor on the laboratory wall, the one that had displayed Michael and Chief Hughes's voice waveforms earlier. The screen lit up with a whine. 'Just tuning this into your records, commander. Won't be a sec.'

The holographic solar system appeared upon it.

'That's what we saw earlier,' Michael said.

'Yeah, with that mysterious planet,' Hsui added.

'Which broke up about seventy million years ago,' the Doctor said. 'Sending huge chunks of itself swimming across the solar system, becoming various satellites, moons and asteroids. All that remained of a planet teeming with life. One day it was there. The next – *pop!* and it's gone.'

'You mean the Moon is all that remains of it?' asked Sam.

'Possibly. Or maybe the snakes just hitched a lift on your Moon a lot earlier, as it was drifting through space. Either way, they've been here a very long time.'

'And now all they want to do is get home?' asked Sam. 'Can we help them?'

'Scary space snakes?' the Doctor said to him.

Sam looked at the snakes. 'Not so scary really. Just a little sad.'

'I like you, Sam. I really do,' said the Doctor.
'Commander Cann, this lad has a good attitude about
alien species. You should take him on staff.'

'He's only fourteen,' she said.

'Oh. Oh, right. Well then, in a few years. He'll be
an asset.' The Doctor turned back to the leader snake.
'Sorry, it's bad news for you guys. Your home is gone.
Has been for millions and millions of years.'

The leader snake said nothing, but Sam realised he
and the others were all looking towards the computer
screen, staring at the image on it.

The Doctor zapped it again, and the image
changed to a contemporary view of the solar system.
'That's how it is now,' he said.

*Hiss.*

'Possibly,' he said. 'But it would be a dangerous
journey. You might be better off staying local, where
you know you can survive. It would be a waste to get
out there and discover no one else survived. Better to
be the last of your people and live than to die out there
on a fruitless search for others who may be long dead.'

*Hiss.*

'Because, well, because I've never encountered any
of them. Anywhere. And I know this system pretty
well. I'm not saying it's impossible, but I wouldn't
recommend it.'

*Hiss.*

'Well, you just have to negotiate with the lovely commander here. She's very nice, really.'

'Negotiate?' asked Commander Cann. 'I can't speak Snake!'

'Perspective, commander! Communication is a lost art with humans. Learn. Share this Moon, this Moonbase with your neighbours.' The Doctor looked at the leader snake. 'Give her a few minutes to digest this.'

'World State's insurance won't cover all this!' Joe Rivas suddenly yelled. 'Alien snakes and stuff!'

Everyone, including his sister, turned to look at him in shock.

'Perspective,' the Doctor said again, shaking his head.

Jo Rivas led her brother to a seat and sat him down.

'I have to know,' the Doctor said, 'how much World State knew about the snakes. Did they expect this? Were you sent here to observe this?'

'We were sent here to make sure the stupid kids didn't get sucked out of an airlock and to show them where their stupid murals were going to be painted,' Joe Rivas spat angrily. 'Stop assuming that just cos we work for the world's biggest multinational corporation, we are the enemy. We didn't ask to be taken over by snakes.'

The Doctor looked at them both, but clearly decided to believe him. Finally he put the red toolbox down on the floor beside the snakes, who immediately surrounded it.

'Don't touch,' the Doctor barked. 'You have attacked this Moonbase, hurt the crew, siphoned off power that, left unchecked, could have been dangerous to the humans. So, before we get into this, we need to work out a plan.'

'I want to know who this Lukas Minski is and what his connection to the snakes is,' said Chief Christoffel. 'You know, as Chief of Security. Sort of thing I ought to know, isn't it?'

The Doctor smiled. 'Let me tell you what I reckon. Lukas faked his death, his disappearance, because of whatever he put inside this toolbox. He didn't want UNIT getting their hands on it again. He was very brave to do what he did. Lukas worked in a UNIT museum, dealing with things that made him sad because they were often stolen.'

*Hissss.*

The Doctor sighed and looked at the leader snake. 'Well, okay, if you know the story, smartypants, why not tell it yourself instead of leaving me to work it all out – brilliantly, I have to say. I'm on the right track, aren't I?'

*Hissss.*

'Oh, right, well there you are then!' He turned to the others. 'Solved.'

'Doctor?' said Commander Cann slowly.

'What now?'

'We don't understand Snake.'

'Ah, yes, right. Got you. Okay, very simple. UNIT steal alien stuff. Providing it's not weaponry, they put it in a museum, probably utterly unaware of what it is. Enter Lukas Minski, not a rich man, not terribly honest – he nicks something. Gets fired, ends up working here on the Moon, far away from the authorities on Earth. Meets the snakes – they're drawn to him because he's been in contact with something they have been looking for, well, for a few thousand, possibly million years. My Snake translation is a bit rusty, but I'm plumping for millions. Lukas talks to the snakes –'

'How?' asked Hsui.

'As I said, been in contact with something of theirs. Quick bite on the hand and bingo! Instant communication between the two minds – leader snake here, Lukas Minski there.'

The Doctor tapped a code into the red toolbox's lid and the box opened.

As many people as possible clustered round the box, making sure they didn't tread on any snakes.

'A golden egg?' said Christoffel.

The Doctor nodded. 'A golden egg. Yes.'

He looked around but no one seemed to understand.

And then Sam did. 'Snakes,' he said. 'Snakes hatch from eggs.'

The Doctor beamed. 'That's not a weapon or even a looted work of art. That's the egg of a snake queen, or something similar, anyway – could be a king. But that's what that is. Give it to the snakes and everyone can go home.'

'So Lukas made a deal with them,' Sam said slowly, piecing it together. 'He would get them their egg back.'

The Doctor nodded. 'So he went to Earth secretly, got it back eventually – I doubt doing that was entirely above the law – and brought it to the Moon, but the snakes were gone by then. Hiding. World State had moved in, all that change, so they went to ground. Literally. Lukas hid it in the one place no one was working on, no one was redesigning: HEART.'

Sam looked at the way the snakes were staring at the egg, mesmerised. 'They just want to go home to a planet they know is gone. How sad,' he said.

'Doctor, you suggested they stay here, yeah?' asked Commander Cann.

*Hisss.*

'They think you'll kill them,' the Doctor replied.

Commander Cann turned to the leader snake. 'Not going to happen. Ever. Whatever has happened in the past, whatever mistakes were made by the removal of your egg, I apologise on behalf of, well, everyone. This is as much your home as ours. Hell, it's more yours, and you surely can make use of the ninety per cent we haven't built a Moonbase on. Please, stay. It would be so good to live and work together and learn about one another.'

'Are you sure?' the Doctor said.

'Absolutely,' said the commander. 'Why, aren't you?'

The Doctor laughed. 'No, no. I'm just delighted to hear you say that.'

He passed the egg to the snakes, who hissed delightedly.

'Yes,' the Doctor said. 'Look after it better this time, and when it's ready to hatch let the humans know. It'll be a great moment for both of your species.'

'Is the egg okay?' asked Sam. 'I mean, it's been in a toolbox for almost ten years.'

'It's been an egg on the Moon for a few million years before that. I'm pretty sure it's designed to cope,' said the Doctor.

'When is it due to hatch?' Hughes asked.

The Doctor shrugged. 'Probably not in any of your lifetimes.' He looked at Sam. 'Well, maybe yours.'

Joe and Jo Rivas moved to Aaron. 'Did you film all this?' they asked quietly. 'This is going to be huge! You were attacked by the space snakes. Give World State that footage and you'll be a superstar! You could end up the biggest star on the planet!'

Aaron took the camera off his cap and pressed a small switch: the bluetooth connection. 'Actually, I've erased everything that's been shot so far this trip,' he said quietly. 'No snakes, no attacks, no egg. Nothing. Tomorrow, we can start again, with the guys here and their murals and everything.'

'Are you mad?' Joe Rivas exploded. 'The snake footage is worth ten times some stupid pictures drawn by kids.' He turned to Sam. 'No offence.'

'Lots taken, actually,' said Sam.

Jo Rivas was slightly less hysterical than her brother. 'No back-ups, Aaron?'

'All erased. You're too late,' said Aaron, smiling. 'Can you imagine what would happen if World State knew about the space snakes? They'd be up here, dissecting them or something. The snakes should stay the Moon's secret. That's why I've erased it all.'

Joe Rivas shrugged. 'So? We'll tell them what went on. They'll be up here to investigate in a matter of days.'

Aaron shrugged. 'But, with no footage to back up your claims, why would they believe you?'

'Because everyone here has seen them!' Joe Rivas turned to the Moonbase Laika staff. 'You all work for World State. It's your job to tell them about the space snakes.'

'What space snakes?' asked Commander Cann. 'Anyone know anything about any space snakes?'

'Sounds like a mad old story to me,' said Llewellyn Hughes.

'No idea what Mr Rivas is talking about,' said Godfried Christoffel.

'Just as well,' the Doctor said. 'Look.'

All but one of the snakes had gone. Slithered silently away, carrying the egg, their heritage.

The leader snake was still there, swaying slightly as it seemed to weigh up its options.

*Hisss.*

It slithered away into the ventilation system before anyone could move.

'They'll be in touch,' the Doctor said simply. 'Don't let them down.' He smiled at Commander Cann. 'Don't let me down.'

# Chapter 16

# Alive and Kicking

Sam was at home on Earth in his back garden. His parents were shopping and he was sitting in the sunshine, reading a book about snakes.

The *BPXtra* shows had gone out. Moonbase Laika was decorated with all the murals. Aaron Relevy had struck a deal to regularly do shows from the Moon about life up there, with Hsui as a co-host (and, Sam reckoned, a bit more). Caitlin, Michael and especially Savannah had all stayed in touch with him. Four friends for life.

He wondered if he'd ever see the Doctor again.

As if in answer, the doorbell rang and he went to answer it.

The Doctor was there, grinning. 'Hello, Sam, glad I didn't miss you. Last time I knocked, you'd got an

engineering degree, married Savannah, moved
to Switzerland and this place was occupied by a
strange old lady with twelve cats.' He stopped.
'Probably shouldn't have told you that – the future's a
funny old thing. Anyway, glad you're still here and
still fourteen years old. Got someone who wants to
say hello.'

He moved aside and Sam could see an old man
standing by the gate.

It was the same old man he'd met before, back at
the *BPXtra* studios, although he was better dressed
now. He was even wearing a bow tie. Clearly he'd been
out shopping with the Doctor.

They shook hands, and Lukas Minski started to
thank Sam for everything he'd done to get the egg
back to the snakes. 'You were magnificent, according
to the Doctor. Very brave.'

The Doctor smiled. 'We're heading back to
Georgia tomorrow – his family is so excited that they
are going to be reunited. And I pulled a few strings
with UNIT to clear his name.'

'After so many years, I can see them again. They
thought I was dead. My Annika will be all grown up.
I have missed so much of her life.'

'Anyway, we just wanted to say bye and thank you,'
the Doctor said.

'Hang on,' said Sam. 'When we were leaving Moonbase Laika, Commander Cann gave me something, in case we ever met again, Mr Minski.'

Sam rushed up to his bedroom, pulled out a box from under his bed and headed back down to the door. He passed it over.

'She said you might want it.'

Frowning, Lukas opened the box.

It was a home-made moon buggy, next to a card in Lukas's handwriting that read:

*To my beloved daughter, Annika. Happy tenth birthday.*

'Thank you,' Lukas said quietly. 'Better late than never.' He gave Sam a huge hug. 'For everything.'

Lukas Minski walked back down the path, tightly holding the box containing Annika's gift.

The Doctor shook Sam's hand. 'Goodbye for now. I look forward to meeting you again in Switzerland. Something to do with solving the Oil Apocalypse, I seem to recall. We make a great team. Or did. Or will. Whatever.'

And he was gone.

Sam knew that it wouldn't be the last time he saw the Doctor.

Because life was good like that.

## The End

# Titles in the series:

The Galactic Fair has arrived on the mining asteroid of Stanalan and anticipation is building around the construction of the fair's most popular attraction – the Death Ride! But there is something sinister going on behind all the fun of the fair: people are mysteriously dying in the Off-Limits tunnels. Join the Doctor, Amy and Rory as they investigate . . .

The Doctor finds himself trapped in the virtual world of Parallife. As the Doctor tries to save the inhabitants from being destroyed by a deadly virus, Amy and Rory must fight to keep his body in the real world, safe from the mysterious entity known as Legacy . . .

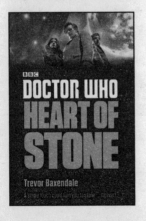

The Doctor, Amy and Rory are surprised to discover lumps of moon rock scattered around a farm. But things get even stranger when they find out where the moon rock is coming from – a Rock Man is turning everything he touches to stone! Can the Doctor, Amy and Rory find out what the creature wants before it's too late?

The Eleventh Doctor and his friends, Amy and Rory, join a group of explorers on a Victorian tramp steamer in the Florida Everglades. The mysterious explorers are searching for the Fountain of Youth, but neither they – nor the treasure they seek – are quite what they seem...

Terrible tiny creatures swarm down from the sky, intent on destroying everything on planet Xirrinda. As the colonists try to fight the alien infestation, the Eleventh Doctor searches for the ancient secret weapon of the native Ulla people. Is it enough to save the day?

A distress signal calls the TARDIS to the *Black Horizon*, a spaceship under attack from the Empire of Eternal Victory. But the robotic scavengers are the least of the Eleventh Doctor's worries. Something terrifying is waiting to trap him in space...

The Eleventh Doctor treats Rory to a trip
to the Wild West, where the TARDIS crew find
a town full of sleeping people and a gang of
menacing outlaws intent on robbing the local
bank. But it soon becomes clear that Amy,
Rory and the Doctor are not the only
visitors to Mason City, Nevada . . .

An ancient artefact awakes, trapping one
of the Eleventh Doctor's companions on an
archaeological dig in Egypt. The only way
for the Doctor to save his friend is to travel
thousands of years back in time to defeat
the mysterious Water Thief . . .

People are mysteriously disappearing
on Moonbase Laika. They eventually return,
but with strange bite marks on their bodies
and no idea where they have been.
Can the Eleventh Doctor get to the
bottom of what's going on?

# Your story starts here . . .

Do you **love books** and **discovering new stories**? Then **www.puffin.co.uk** is the place for you . . .

- Thrilling adventures, fantastic fiction and laugh-out-loud fun

- Brilliant videos featuring your favourite authors and characters

- Exciting competitions, news, activities, the Puffin blog and SO MUCH more . . .

www.puffin.co.uk

 # Listen

## Do you love listening to stories?

## Want to know what happens behind the scenes in a recording studio?

Hear funny sound effects, exclusive author interviews and the best books read by famous authors and actors on the **Puffin Podcast** at **www.puffin.co.uk**

# #ListenWithPuffin

them here and set them on the judges' table."

A boy with a big number one on his T-shirt put his sneakers on the table and stepped back.

Colin was checking out the rest of the contestants. Some he knew from school. Number four he'd never seen before, and number five! Number five was Poppy Roginski. She was wearing pink shorts and a pink-and-white-striped top. Her black hair was held back with a pink-and-white-polka-dotted hairband. Colin thought she was as pretty as an Easter egg. On her feet were the nastiest-looking sneakers he'd ever seen in his life. Maybe they'd been white once. Now they were a moldering, festering, disgusting black.

Vaguely Colin heard his mother ask, "Would you and Amy like to go straight home and take a bath? Webbie, you, too?"

"I'd like to stay and watch the contest," Colin said.

"You've got to be kidding . . ." Webster began. And then he said, "Oh-oh. Look who's number five. It's Poppy Roginski!"

"Now I see why we've got to stay for the competition," Amy added.

The five of them walked across the grass. There were two men judges, one bald, one with a mustache. The other judge was a woman wearing a Mickey Mouse sweatshirt. Another man stood a little apart from the other three. He was dressed in a three-piece suit, vest and all.

"Number five," the woman judge called out.

Poppy lifted her feet free of her unlaced abominations and carried her sneakers up to the table.

The woman judge leaned toward her, then wafted a piece of paper across her own face as if she needed air.

"Our young lady contestant here says

she wears her sneakers when she's mucking out her duck house on their farm," she called to the audience. "And I certainly believe her."

There was a ripple of laughter from the crowd as Poppy put her sneakers on the table and the two other judges pretended to faint.

That was when Poppy Roginski looked up and smiled at Colin. Smiled right at him. She was wearing her special-occasion pink braces on her teeth and her cheeks were pink, too. She was dazzling.

Colin thought he might faint himself.

# sixteen

"I SEE BRUNO and Mr. Sabaton," Amy said, and she crouched down and called, "Bruno! Bruno, come!"

He came, furiously pulling Mr. Sabaton across the grass.

"Look! It's Jack Dunn's turn," Mom said.

Number eleven was strutting to the table where the other pairs of stinky sneakers sat in a numbered row. Each time the breeze wafted in their direction Colin could smell the blend of them. It was like the time a rat had died in the basement of their building. They hadn't found it for six days. When anyone had opened the basement door, pee-ew!

Jack Dunn set his sneakers on the end of the table and the bald-headed judge propped the number eleven behind them.

"My word!" The judge whipped out a large white handkerchief and held it to his nose. "Are those rotten eggs I smell?"

Jack Dunn smiled. "No, those are my sneakers."

The judge with the mustache gave them a cautious sniff. "A wonderful odor of decay," he said.

"He's going to win," Webster whispered glumly.

The woman judge poked the sneakers with her pencil, then lifted one with the pencil point and examined it, but not too closely. "Why the smell of rotten eggs?"

"Well, you see, ma'am, I live on a farm. It's my job to go out to the hen-house and gather the eggs for my mother. Sometimes I accidentally stand on one or two."

Colin rolled his eyes.

"Jack Dunn lives on Fourth Street," he whispered to his dad.

"Isn't that a fish smell, too?" the woman judge asked.

"Yes, ma'am. A river runs through our back field. Sometimes fish jump out, you know? Flying fish? And we don't see them. That's why my sneakers smell so great," Jack finished. "All natural."

"What a liar," Webster said.

"What a jerk," Amy added.

The mustached judge had the mega-phone now. "Well, number eleven is our final contestant. We'll take a few minutes now to make our very difficult decision."

Jack Dunn strutted back to his place in the line.

"Let's jump him," Webster suggested. "Let's make him eat his rotten, cheating sneakers. You and Amy could do it. I could be the lookout in case Shrike the Terrible tries to—"

"It's going to be a close call," Colin's dad said, and Colin's mom leaned across and whispered, "We're proud of you, Colin, for what you did."

Colin smiled at her. Yeah, he thought, but no new sneakers for us. It was as if his mom read his thoughts. She could do that sometimes. "You wanted to win for us as much as for yourself. But as far as we're concerned, you're a winner now."

"Hear, hear," Mr. Sabaton said. He unhooked the leash and Bruno found another dog running free and played tag with it around the oak tree.

Colin secretly watched Jack Dunn sneak up behind Poppy Roginski and pull off her pink-and-white-polka-dotted hairband. He watched Poppy plead with him to give it back. Jack Dunn put the band on his own greasy hair, low on his forehead like he was a surfer or a tennis player. Like he was the stinky-sneaker king already.

The music stopped as abruptly as it had started and the woman judge took the megaphone. "This has been a tough decision," she said. "We have perfect examples of offensiveness here. One pair of sneakers is just about as foul as the next. But it is the unanimous decision of the judges that number five, Miss Poppy Roginski, is the winner."

"Yeah! Super!" Everyone was applauding.

Webster grabbed Colin's arm. "This is great. Poppy likes us. Who needs three pairs of sneakers? Maybe she'll give you a pair and me a pair and—"

"Dream on, Webster," Colin's dad said.

"Mr. Dunker, owner of the Slam Dunker Stores and sponsor of this competition, will award the prize," the woman judge shouted.

The man in the three-piece suit walked across the grass during the cheering, took Poppy's hand, and escorted her to the table.

Colin thought Mr. Dunker was the luckiest guy on earth. He thought Poppy Roginski was just like Miss America getting her crown, except that Poppy Roginski was prettier and smaller.

Jack Dunn sat on the grass wiggling his toes. He'd thrown Poppy Roginski's pink-and-white-polka-dotted hairband on the grass in front of him.

Cameras flashed and the crowd cheered as Poppy accepted the gift certificate and went back in line with the rest of the contestants.

"She just got it 'cause she's a girl and she's cute," Jack Dunn yelled.

—— crowd yelled. "Boo, bad sport."

And Colin couldn't believe what he was doing himself, either. He must have left his brains behind in the garbage truck. He was hurrying over to Jack Dunn as fast as his stiff-legged jeans would let him walk.

Jack Dunn looked up when Colin stopped in front of him.

"You just shut up, Jack Dunn," Colin said. "Poppy Roginski won fair and square. You didn't, and that was fair and square, too."

"You little weasel," Jack Dunn said.

"Weasel yourself," Colin told him. "You and I will have another chance next year, and so help me, if you try any of that fish-and-egg-stuff again, I'll make you eat your cheating sneakers."

Jack Dunn stood up. "Oh, yeah? You and who?"